THE DEVLIN QUICK MYSTERIES

DIGGING FOR TROUBLE

LINDA FAIRSTEIN

DIAL BOOKS
FOR YOUNG READERS

Dial Books for Young Readers
Penguin Young Readers Group
An imprint of Penguin Random House LLC
375 Hudson Street
New York, NY 10014

Printed in the United States of America

Library of Congress Cataloging-in-Publication Data

Names: Fairstein, Linda A., author.
Title: Digging for trouble / Linda Fairstein.
Description: New York, NY : Dial Books for Young Readers, [2017] | Series: The Devlin Quick mysteries
Identifiers: LCCN 2016057551 | ISBN 9780399186462 (hardback)
Subjects: | CYAC: Mystery and detective stories. | Archaeology—Fiction. | Fossils—Fiction. | Montana—Fiction. | BISAC: JUVENILE FICTION / Mysteries & Detective Stories. | JUVENILE FICTION / Law & Crime. | JUVENILE FICTION / Animals / Dinosaurs & Prehistoric Creatures.
Classification: LCC PZ7.1.F346 Di 2017 | DDC [Fic]—dc23 LC record available at https://lccn.loc.gov/2016057551

1 3 5 7 9 10 8 6 4 2

Design by Mina Chung • Text set in Chapparel Pro

FOR NANCY DREW

AND FOR JOE AND FRANK HARDY,

who taught me everything I needed to

know about sleuthing

1

"I think I'm afraid to keep digging, Dev," Katie said.

We were both on our hands and knees, crawling up the side of a gulch in Montana, somewhere between the Great Plains and the Rocky Mountains. I turned over and sat up, reaching for a bottle of water from my backpack.

"You haven't got any reason to be afraid, Katie," I said. "Take a sip and chill out."

It was 94 degrees in the middle of the afternoon, and there was nothing—no trees, no bushes or shrubs—nothing to offer any shade to us as we inched forward over the brown sandstone surface of the hill.

"I don't want to be touching anybody's bones," Katie said, brushing off her hands. "That would really creep me out."

"It's not people we're looking for. It's fossils," I said. "Trust me, I'm not interested in coming face-to-face with human bones, either."

"Then why are you working so hard at this?"

I had a small hammer and a whisk broom, sort of a

handheld miniature version of a large sweeper, sticking out of my pants pockets. I had been using both of them—one to poke at rock formations and the other to brush away the dirt that covered them—as I made my way up the steep incline.

"C'mon, Katie. You like a good adventure as much as I do. There are supposed to be dinosaur fossils all over this valley," I said, sweeping my arm around in a semicircle, taking in the vast expanse of what the locals called Big Sky Country. "Isn't it cool to think we might find some of them?"

"Don't even mention the word 'cool,'" Katie said, holding the water bottle against her forehead. "I think I was six years old when my dad bought our ranch out here in Big Timber. I never figured Montana doesn't have an ocean anywhere around it. I really miss the beach right now."

"If you paid attention in science last year, you'd remember that where we're sitting this very moment was once the sea," I said, reaching over to fan my best friend with my whisk broom. "The Cretaceous Western Interior Seaway, right next to the coastal plains where gigantic dinosaurs roamed seventy million years ago."

"I can't believe that you actually did homework to prepare for this summer vacation trip," Katie said, rolling her eyes at me. "That is so Devlin Quick of you."

"I *am* Devlin Quick," I said, getting to my feet and giving Katie my hand to help her up. "Besides, your dad signed us up for this dino dig, and we've only got two more days to go. I'm getting fossil fever, for sure."

Katie Cion and I met in kindergarten. We were starting eighth grade at the Ditchley School in Manhattan—a private girls' school—after summer break. We were pretty much inseparable, and I was so happy her parents had invited me to spend two weeks at their ranch.

"Now what?" Katie asked.

"We've got a couple more hours to go," I said. "We have to reach that tent at the top of the ridge by five o'clock, for everyone to check in on the day's progress."

"Why isn't there a ski lift to get me up there, Dev? My legs are too short for this climb."

I was back on my hands and knees, trying to concentrate on unusual spots on the surface of the ground. "Think of it this way, Katie. Your very cute neighbor will be waiting at the peak, and I've seen the way you look at that cowboy."

"Kyle? You're ridiculous, Dev. He's just my Montana buddy," Katie said. "And he's fourteen years old. I mean, he's not interested in me."

Katie was back in position with her head just inches

above the top layer of earth, probably so that I couldn't see her blush. She was pawing away at the dirt with renewed enthusiasm.

The land we were digging on was privately owned. It was a few miles away from Big Timber, which is the town where Katie's dad had built a ranch on the Boulder River. He liked to go fly-fishing, and the river that roared through the Cion's backyard was perfect for that.

"What do you think this is?" Katie asked, holding up a round gray object that looked like an ordinary rock.

"I have no idea. Why not wrap it in that soft material they gave us and put it in your backpack to show to Mr. Paulson?"

Steve Paulson was the man who was supervising the dig. He was a paleontologist—a scientist who studies fossils. The government doesn't fund much of this work, so Steve told Katie's dad that he liked to have volunteers to help him with summer digs.

About nine months ago, the rancher who lives on the land we were on today, found the giant leg bone of a dinosaur. He had just been out hiking on a path that went from his property into the state forest next to it when he spotted it.

Steve met with all the volunteers last night to explain

what we'd be doing and what we should look for. He told us he was pretty certain that the remote acres of land on the Double G Ranch were actually a bone bed—a dense deposit of fossil bones from prehistoric times.

Katie stopped and removed a length of light-brown padding from her pack. "This really smells gross," she said, wrapping the rock inside it and tucking it away.

"It's made from the hair of a camel," I said. "It's called camel matting. It's what they use in the desert to protect things they find there, like your piece of rock, because it's so soft."

"Cotton's soft, too, and it doesn't smell like it's been sweating in the desert sun for hundreds of years."

"Stop whining about everything, Katie," I said. "Get back to work."

Katie readjusted her hat. She was fair-skinned and blond, and needed to keep covered from the sun. I had black hair like my dad and a complexion that tanned easily, though both Katie and I had lathered up with sunscreen. Katie was petite and at least four inches shorter than me. I was what my grandmother liked to call a "gangly girl"—long-legged and lanky.

I scraped away loose dirt in hopes of finding buried treasure. Every now and then, I looked back over my shoulder to check out what the others were doing. Some were working by themselves, while others formed small clusters on the broad hillside.

I must have been ten or twelve feet ahead of Katie.

"Why are you going so fast?" she said to me. "I don't want you to leave me behind. Don't you know what the Double G stands for?"

"You mean the name of this ranch?" I asked. "Clue me in."

"My dad says the initials stand for Great Grizzlies, Dev. Like this land is totally covered in bears. That's what the place was named for."

I paused and looked back at Katie, laughing at her. "Not right here, that's for sure. Bears don't like the heat. They spend this part of the day sleeping in some shaded grassy spot. They're more likely to be under the cottonwood trees along the river in your backyard in Big Timber than where we are now."

I continued my climb up the slope, even though I was losing my patience. It was tough work to comb the ground for bits and pieces of stuff. I didn't realize how far I had gotten from Katie until I heard her shout my name out loud.

"Devlin!"

I stood up and glanced down at her, now thirty feet away.

"What is it?"

Katie's voice had carried across the hillside and almost everyone stopped in his or her tracks to look over at her.

I ran down, slipping as I neared my friend and landing on my tail. "What is it? Are you all right?"

"I'm fine. I'm perfectly fine."

There was a small bump protruding from the sandstone, covered in gnarled pebbles and sharp pieces of rock. Next to that were a few strips of gray-black stone that almost looked like fingers. Human fingers.

I let out a low whistle. "I bet they're dinosaur bones," I said. "They look exactly like the photographs Mr. Paulson showed us last night."

"The color is right," Katie said, almost shivering with excitement. "The size and shape are the same. They could be remains from small dinosaurs, couldn't they?"

Katie took a few more pieces of camel matting out of her pack and began to wrap the three pieces she had found. "This mat smells like perfume to me now."

I reached into my bag and pulled out the small can of orange-neon paint, spraying a large circle around the area to mark the spot of Katie's find, like Steve had taught us to do this morning.

Neither one of us heard the approach of the man until

he stood over us, the brim of his cowboy hat casting a shadow over my hand and the tip of his hiking boots practically stepping on the spray-painted marking I'd made.

"What have you got there, little lady?" he asked in a Montana drawl.

"Just some rocks, I think," Katie said, always fast-thinking on her feet. "I'm picking them up to give to Mr. Paulson when we get to the crest."

"Why don't you show them to me?" he said, holding out his hand to her.

"I don't know you, sir. I was told to hold everything until Mr. Paulson gets a chance to look at stuff first. I'm sure they're nothing at all."

The man crouched beside us. He was probably fifty or so. His skin was weathered and lined, and his outstretched hand was bigger than a catcher's mitt.

"I'm Chip Donner. I work for Steve Paulson," he said, turning his eyes to me. "Nobody draws a neon circle on the ground around nothin', missy, do they? So why not just show me what you two found?"

Katie looked to me and I nodded. "Let him see, Katie. No harm in that."

She slowly unrolled her three little packages and set them back on the ground. Chip Donner glanced at the odd-looking pieces. He didn't crack a smile. I had no idea what he was thinking.

"Just rocks," he said. "You girls will learn soon enough. I thought maybe you had something real good, like a dinosaur tooth."

"We're pretty happy with these for right now," Katie said. "Whatever they are."

"Tell you what—Miss—?"

"Cion. Katie Cion."

"So you're David Cion's kid?" Donner said, reaching underneath the trio of camel mats with his huge hand and standing tall to hold them up over our heads, before I could get to my feet to challenge him. "Why don't I just help you out, for your daddy's sake? I'll walk these right up to the tent and make sure they get tagged and photographed and returned to you by the time you reach the top."

"We don't need help," I said. "Thanks very much but we're doing just fine."

"Wouldn't want you breaking up things in the event they have value," he said. "I wouldn't want you to get blamed for splitting these rocks in half in case you slip down again and fall on top of them."

"Katie's the most responsible girl I know," I said, but Donner was walking away from me faster than I could go, and Katie was still picking up her supplies from the ground.

"I can't believe I let that guy take off with my fossils, Dev," Katie said. She was close to tears and I understood exactly why.

"Cowgirls don't cry," I said. "The faster we can get to the top, the sooner we blow the whistle on him."

"But my bones," Katie said.

I grabbed her hand and started pulling her up the incline. "You didn't want any bones in the first place. Now get moving."

We reached the ridge about twenty minutes later, sweating and out of breath and completely disheartened.

The area under the small white open-sided tent held three tables, one of them set up with lemonade and cookies. The other two seemed to be work sites, where an assortment of specimens were laid out, each one of which was resting on a piece of paper on which the volunteer's name was written. I looked for three pieces the shape of Katie's find, but didn't see anything like them.

Two women were in charge of refreshments. Several of the older volunteers were seated on folding chairs, refreshing themselves, while others were chatting in small groups.

Kyle Lowry, Katie's Big Timber neighbor, was just getting off his dirt bike and ambling over to the tent.

"The worst thing happened to us just now, Kyle," Katie said.

"What's that?"

"Well, I found some things—Dev and I think they might be dinosaur fossils. And I guess I made too much noise, and the next thing I know this guy came down the hill and he took them away from me. Just snatched them and walked off."

"Steve Paulson?"

"No, Kyle," I said. "We met Steve last night. This man said his name is Chip Donner. He spooked both of us, to tell you the truth. Does he really work for Steve?"

"I mean the pieces I found aren't here on the table," Katie said, breaking in to my series of questions. "They're just gone."

"Don't get panicky, Katie," Kyle said, pulling his hands out of the pockets of his jeans. "They'll turn up. Donner's not a thief. My dad knows him from back home in Big Timber. Nobody working for Steve would be a thief."

"What do we do?" I asked. I felt sort of out of place here. Back in Manhattan, I was a lot surer of myself. "Should we ask Steve about this?"

"I don't think so," Katie said. "Not yet, anyway. I

don't want to bother him unless I'm really certain of everything."

"Whatever you think," I said. "I know who to go to for help when I'm at home, but this territory feels like being on a different planet."

"You're in the Badlands, Dev. The Montana Badlands," Kyle Lowry said. "Let's all just stick together. These parts didn't get that name for no reason."

2

Kyle was waiting for us outside our tent, a pretty shabby structure which held our own sleeping bags and two others, to take us to Steve's evening meeting. Katie and I had put on bathing suits and jumped into a freezing cold pocket in the nearby river—our excuse for a shower—then eaten dinner with the other volunteers around a campfire.

"I'm beginning to think this is your fault, Dev," Katie said, pulling on her hiking boots again as I brushed my wet hair up into a ponytail.

"What is?"

"Things disappear right under your nose lately," she said. "That rare map from the library and now—"

"A thief stole that map, Katie," I said. "Liza and I helped find it. You weren't even around when it happened, so don't say ridiculous things."

"Well, you let Mr. Donner walk off with my bones."

"I did no such thing," I said, lifting the flap to leave the tent. "You didn't exactly rise to the occasion, Katie.

And as my grandmother would say, 'I'm not done with Mr. Donner yet.'"

I let her catch up with Kyle and followed behind them. Most of the adults were gathered around fire pits, talking and exchanging stories with one another.

Steve Paulson's headquarters was an enormous teepee—not a camping tent like ours. It was held up by four pine poles, more than twenty feet high, which crossed one another and interlocked at the top, and were covered on the sides by canvas. It was so big that inside there were even carpets and oversize pillows scattered on the floor. Six of the older kids were relaxing after the long day's work.

Steve had actually built a campfire in the middle of the teepee, and one of his assistants was fixing up some s'mores for us to roast over it.

"Give a welcome to Katie and Dev," Steve said. "Kyle's sort of a summer regular here. The rest of you should introduce yourselves."

Most of the others—five guys and a girl—were college and graduate students. One of them, a very slender young woman, got up and came over to Katie and me.

"Hi. My name is Ling," she said, shaking my hand. "I'm in grad school at Yale University. I'll be one of your tentmates tonight."

I perked up at the chance to talk to an older girl who was enough of a brainiac to be at Yale, and also had come a long way to offer to help with the dig. "Sweet," I said. "That'll be fun."

Katie had two older brothers. I was the only child of a single mother and had always wanted a sibling. A couple of years ago, my mom sort of adopted a teenager who'd been orphaned. Now Natasha, who was twenty-two, was part of our family.

"Sit yourselves down, please, and make yourselves at home," Steve said. "I like to get us together every evening because the questions you have now—after spending your first day in the field and getting your hands in the dirt—are going to be a lot better than the ones you asked me yesterday."

"Yeah," Katie whispered to me, "like where are my bones? That's a good question, isn't it?"

"Don't go there yet," I said. "Let's scope out the situation, okay?"

"I began my first dig in northwest Montana," Steve said. "On Blackfoot Territory. This teepee is modeled after the original Blackfoot ones, perfected over hundreds of years. Tall, airy, full of light and sturdy, too. Holds a good fire in here."

The woman helping Steve was holding s'mores over

the flames and passing out the sticks with melted marshmallow and chocolate to each of us.

"What's the first question you should be asking?" Steve said.

Nobody raised a hand.

"No time to be shy," he said. "Why are we here? I mean right here on the Double G Ranch today?"

Katie whispered again, reminded of grizzlies when Steve mentioned the name of the ranch. "Did you say bears come out at night mostly?"

"I did. Nocturnal in this heat."

"Then why *are* we here right now? We could be back at my place hunkered down with a good movie and cell service, texting everyone at home in New York City."

"Sometimes you are so narrow-minded, Katie." I pinched her arm. There was no cell service at all on this remote hilltop. "Remember the Ditchley motto: 'We Learn, We Lead.' You've got to stay out in front of things. Take some dares every now and then. Be bold."

"What's there to lead, Dev? Dinos have been extinct for seventy million years, give or take a few million. That path is taking me nowhere I need to go."

A guy with a beard—a student at Montana State University—spoke up. "I'm here, Steve, because I want to learn from the best, and I know that's you."

Steve Paulson waved off the compliment. "What else?"

"So, the ranch owner found this piece of a dinosaur leg—a femur, right?"

"Yep. The femur is the thighbone, longest and strongest in the human body—likely the same in dinosaurs—from the hip to the knee."

"But why have you waited almost a year to do our dig?"

I was chowing down on my s'mores, thinking that was a good question.

"Several reasons for that," Steve said. "First off, it was winter when we got a confirmed ID on the fact that the femur was from a dino. And winter is no time to dig in central Montana. Since the discovery was made on private property, it was pretty easy to secure the area against trespassers. Foul weather and trespassers are the two biggest enemies of my work, young man."

"Understood."

"Then we had to get all the legal permits," Steve said. "Fossils found on government property remain just that."

"What do you mean?" I asked.

"A lot of the land out here is public property, monitored by the United States Forest Service. So they get to be in charge of any dinosaur bones people come across there."

"But what about the fossils that are right on this hillside?" I said.

"Well, if you happen to dig up a triceratops horn under your tent tonight," Steve said, "that belongs to the owner of the Double G. You'd be negotiating with him to carry it off into the sunset with you."

"Tell that to Chip Donner," Katie said, a little too loud for my liking. "I can't believe those precious little bones could have been my very own."

"They're not your very own," I said while Steve took a sip from a bottle of water. "Didn't you just hear him?"

"You bet. But my dad knows this ranch owner," Katie said. "I'm hoping that if I ask really, really nicely that he'll let me—or you and Kyle—keep at least some of what we find. And who knows? Maybe he's allergic to dinosaurs."

"Third thing," Steve said, "is that I tried to get some satellite imagery from space."

My "wow" was audible to everyone in the tent.

"There are a few places on earth that have been rich in fossil deposits, because that's where the land was suitable for dinosaurs to live at the time. Alberta, up in Canada, is one of them, and Argentina is another—"

My turn to cover my mouth and speak to Katie. "Liza's from Argentina, you know," I said. Liza was an exchange student who had just spent three weeks living with me and my mom to go to the Ditch summer program. "I wonder if she's more interested in dinos than you."

"Don't go threatening to switch besties on me, Dev."

"For me," Mr. Paulson said, "it's been all about Montana. Not far from where we are tonight, in Billings, is where the first juveniles—the first baby dinosaur fossils—were found, not all that long ago. They're rarer than you can imagine. That's kind of what I'm hoping to find right here. Fossils of babies, dinosaur eggs of any kind, and even the nests themselves."

Kyle got up to help himself to another round of s'mores. He poked his stick over the campfire.

I raised my hand. "Mr. Paulson—"

"Just call me Steve. That's what everyone does."

"Okay, Steve. So, someone told me that terrible things happened right here where we are," I said, sort of glaring at Kyle. "That these are the Badlands. So before I have any nightmares, would you mind telling us exactly what's so dangerous about this territory?"

At the same moment that Steve Paulson gave me his most serious expression in return for my question, Kyle tried to suppress a grin.

"Who was filling your head with ideas about danger, Dev?" Steve asked. "The term 'Badlands' doesn't have anything to do with violence."

"Outlaws, then?" I asked, watching Kyle bite his lip and shake the flame off his s'more. "Criminals?"

"No, ma'am. It's a geological expression," Steve said. "Badlands is a name for a kind of terrain that exists out here—in Montana, in the Dakotas, in parts of Wyoming. It refers to land that's been greatly eroded over time by wind and by water. Badlands are soil formations, resulting from deposits of different sorts of clays and silts and sand. Don't you let anyone scare you into thinking this is risky business."

I bit hard into the edge of the plastic cup and my lemonade spilled onto my lap. Kyle suckered me right into that one.

"If it's not about outlaws," Katie said to me, "I'm going to ask Steve where my three bones are when he stops talking, okay?"

"Go for it."

Steve stood up and was pacing around the fire, casting his shadow against the inside of the tall teepee.

"Paleontology—my branch of science—is not an experimental one. I can't test my results in a lab experiment, like a chemist or biologist can."

The older guys were nodding along with Steve.

"This is an historical science. That's why we're going into the field. We test our ideas by exploring the earth, by trying to find old bones—whether from woolly mammoths or lizards or birds—to help us understand the history of life on this planet."

Suddenly, there was another large shadow on the side of the canvas. Chip Donner had just walked into the room. He was holding two small plastic boxes, stacked on top of each other, with both hands.

"Your chance is the opportunity to dig up buried treasure, because that's what these fossils are," Steve said. He was fired up now, with the passion of a great explorer. "If you are fortunate enough to pick up a fragment of bone, you know you'll be holding something that was alive many millions of years before mankind even existed."

"That's an awesome thought," Katie said.

I was listening, but my eyes were glued on Chip.

"And whether what you hold in your hand is a vertebra of a familiar dinosaur, or something from an entirely new species, you will be the very first human being to see that particular piece of prehistoric life. Just think of that."

The older students were buzzing among themselves.

Chip Donner approached Steve Paulson and said something to him, passing over the boxes.

"This is mighty good timing," Steve said. "Thanks to my friend Chip. He's been sorting through all the rocks and pebbles and debris that people picked up along the site today, and it looks like two of you struck gold."

Katie clamped her hand on my crossed leg.

"Ling Soo," he said, "apparently you found a tooth. An intact tooth."

Everyone in the teepee started to clap.

"That's really an important find, Ling, because as those of you who were here a few days ago know, two other volunteers found teeth just a dozen feet away."

"Thank you," Ling said. "I was really excited."

"That suggests there may actually be a full jawbone close by, so it gives us some good energy to go back out into the heat tomorrow," Steve said. "Teeth are also the tools by which we figure out whether the species they came from ate meat—other dinos—or ate berries and other foliage. Think of it all like a detective story, like a mystery that we have to solve once we have all the missing pieces."

I was right on top of it, even before Steve described the hunt as a detective story. Solving crimes was my thing. I loved being a sleuth. It was in my DNA.

"Come get your tooth," Chip said, holding one of the boxes out to Ling. "Sleep with this next to your pillow. When you give it back to Steve tomorrow, it will become a major part of our study going forward."

Ling went up to collect her box and everybody cheered for her.

"Looks like girls rule today," Steve said. "The other discovery was made by our youngest volunteer, Katie Cion."

I threw my arm around her shoulders and shook her till she pushed me off to get to her feet.

"Katie picked up three fossilized bones, and we'll do our work on them but they do appear to be examples of the extremely scarce foot bones of juvenile dinosaurs. The very elusive babies we've been searching for," Steve said. "Pleasant dreams, Katie. Sleep with these beside you."

Katie held the closed box over her head in triumph, like it was a huge silver trophy, and everyone applauded her as she marched back to sit beside me.

"We know these are juvenile," Steve said, "because they're barely three inches long. If they belonged to an adult, they'd be bigger than three feet. Can you imagine that, you guys?"

"What an amazing day," I said as we started to make our way back to our tent. "I'm sticking right by your side tomorrow. I want to find an entire dinosaur's head."

Katie lifted the top of her box and peered down at the three pieces of gray-black bone on the camel matting.

"Hold on a minute, Dev," Katie said. "These aren't the bones Chip Donner took from me a few hours ago. I swear it."

"What do you mean?" I asked.

"We didn't have time to take a photograph of the ones I got, but I know they were longer than this, at least by half an inch."

"You know you can't be sure of that. We didn't examine them so closely."

"Trust me, Dev. Chip switched out my bones for these things," she said, holding them out in front of her like she was allergic to them. "Each one of the three that I found was longer than my own fingers, I know that for sure because I picked each one of them up."

Katie plopped her box on the ground in front of her. "These are as short as my stubby little pinkie."

"Are you certain?" I asked. "Beyond a reasonable doubt?"

My mother had spent a lot of years as a prosecutor in Manhattan. I wasn't allowed to make accusations about people unless I could back them up with evidence.

"Dev, would I try to fool you? My fossils had bits that looked like sockets at one end of the piece that would have connected them to another part of the animal's foot."

"Slow down, Katie. We'll find Steve in the morning and talk to him alone," I said. "You can tell him exactly what you just told me."

She rocked back on her heels, totally dejected and suspicious of this whole operation. "These are just sticks, Dev. Just petrified sticks."

"We won't let Donner get away with this."

"They could have been *my* pieces of buried treasure, Dev. Who'd want to switch something like that out on anyone?"

3

"Keep your distance, Kyle," I said, walking backward and holding out my arm toward him, as Katie and I continued on our way to our tent from Paulson's teepee. "You only fed me that stuff about the Badlands to make fun of me."

"I was just teasing you. Where's your sense of humor, Dev? Did you leave it in the big city?" Kyle asked.

"Actually, I take it with me everywhere I go, just in case someone mean is lurking behind the next butte."

Katie was doubling her steps, trying to keep up with me. "What's a butte, anyway?"

"Sort of a steep hill with a flat top, like the one you see across from your ranch," Kyle said. "Y'all come out here from the East and act like we're characters out of a western movie."

"It's my first time here, Kyle," I said. "I had no idea what to expect."

"Well, I don't know any more about fossils than you do. Sometimes I help Steve out, when he asks me to come on his digs. Mostly I go to school, I play on the football team, I fly-fish on the river like Katie's dad, and I help my dad feed the animals on our farm."

The land in Big Timber was really beautiful. It wasn't dry like this hilltop we were digging on. The Cion ranch and Kyle's family's farm were in a valley. A lot of the farmers, like Kyle's dad, irrigated their land with water from the river, so that alfalfa could grow there to feed the cattle. It was green and lush in the summertime, and when you looked up, you could see snowcapped mountains all around.

"Do you ever ride your horse up into the mountains?" I asked.

"Yeah. Sometimes I just want to get away from my chores and my homework."

Katie had the dopiest look on her face. I thought she was going to swoon at the image of Kyle saddling up his stallion to head for his secret place on the trail above Big Timber.

"There can't be a more serene part of the country than where you live," I said. "We can't even see stars in Manhattan."

I looked overhead and it was as though the entire Milky Way was painted onto the night sky, close enough for me to touch.

"I remember that," Kyle said. "My family spent

Thanksgiving week at Katie's home two years ago. The city lights are so bright that we couldn't see any stars overhead. I didn't like that much."

Kyle veered off to the right and Katie started to follow him. I grabbed the cuff of her sweater and yanked on it, pulling her back toward me.

"Where are you going?" I asked.

Katie just smiled at me sheepishly.

"You guys go to the tent," Kyle said. "I'll get a few bottles of water and flashlights from the supply truck for each of us."

Katie and I went inside and each sat down on our sleeping bags, which had been unfolded by one of the staffers. She didn't seem the least bit interested in her plastic box.

"So what are you going to do about this monster-size crush you have on Kyle when we leave for New York in a few days?" I asked.

"Your mom's right, Dev," Katie said, letting out an exasperated sigh. "You have this tendency to exaggerate everything."

"On the contrary, I have superfine powers of deduction. I mean, I think you two would be good for each other when you're about sixteen," I said. "That is, if you can live on the ranch without Wi-Fi and bodega breakfast sandwiches."

"Time out, Dev!" Katie said, taking off one of her moccasins and tossing it at me.

I ducked and took my moccasins off, too. "Now about the bones."

"Correction. Sticks," Katie said. "Should I let Kyle in on what I'm thinking?"

"That's up to you. He's kind of caught in the middle. Steve's his friend, and he seems to know Chip Donner, too. But then, if he likes you, maybe he can keep a secret for a couple of days, until we figure this out."

"Would you tell Booker Dibble if they were your bones and he was along on the trip?" Katie asked. "He's sort of to you what Kyle is to me."

"That's insane," I said. "Booker is like a brother to me. I've known him longer than I've known you. He's my best guy friend. Practically family. I don't have a crush on Booker. I can't even figure why anyone would have a crush on him."

Katie opened her box and took out one of the three pieces, rolling it over and over in her hands as she eyed it. "Liza did when she was in New York last month. You told me that yourself."

"That's Liza. Don't put her feelings about Booker on me."

The tent flap lifted and Ling ducked under the edge of it to come in. "Way to go, Katie," she said. "Isn't it exciting to make a find?"

"She's thrilled," I said, filling in for Katie's momentary lack of enthusiasm. "Can we have a look at your tooth?"

"Of course," Ling said, bending over to put her box down beside Katie's.

My sleeping bag was head-to-head with Katie's, while the foot of Ling's bag was practically touching the bottom of Katie's. I crawled over to check out the dental specimen.

I opened the plastic box and saw a gigantic tooth, resting on camel matting "That's huge!" I said.

"Isn't it? And it's in perfect condition," Ling said. "You can pick it up."

"What are you going to do with it?" I asked, nervously rubbing the surface of the ancient tooth.

"I'll give it to Steve, of course, for his research project," Ling said. "I just want to have it beside me for the night. Like Steve said, I'm the first human to lay eyes on this fossil."

"Is it the first one you've ever found?" I asked.

"Oh, no. But the first in Montana," Ling said. "I'm from China. I'm just here for graduate school. I've done a whole bunch of digs in the Gobi Desert."

"Mongolia? You've actually been there?"

"Six times. I'm getting my degree in paleontology. The Gobi is one of the most spectacular places in the world," Ling said, and then she laughed. "In fact, there are Mongolian Badlands, just like the territory here. I've dug at Flaming Cliffs, the most famous dinosaur location in the world."

"Where is Mongolia anyway?" Katie asked.

"It's north of China, and south of Russia."

"Katie, I swear, it's like you've forgotten all your geography once summer break started," I said. "Mongolia is totally landlocked. Worse than Montana. It's where Genghis Khan started his empire."

"I'm just distracted," Katie said, tapping on the lid of her plastic box. "Would you trust Mr. Paulson with your treasure, Ling?"

"Of course I would. He's going to be working with a team at the American Museum of Natural History in New York, and I'll be bringing some of the specimens there myself next week."

"We love that museum," I said. "It's the favorite place of every kid in New York."

"It's mine, too," Ling said. "You'll have to come visit me there."

"Listen, Ling," I said, "will you take a look at Katie's bones?"

"I'm happy to do that. I'm not sure I can give you any more information than what you know, just with the naked eye."

"Well, what does your tooth tell you?" I asked. "Steve says a tooth is full of information."

Ling hesitated. "Under a microscope, he'll be able to tease out more important details about these things. He'll be able to compare it to teeth of species that have already been identified."

"But what can you find out without a microscope?" Katie said.

"My first guess is that this animal was a grinder—that he was processing plant food, as opposed to eating meat."

"How would you know that?" I asked.

"Because carnivores—carnosaurs, as we call them—usually have teeth with serrated edges, kind of like steak knives. I can't quite see—"

"Wait a minute," I said, hurrying over to my backpack and extracting my favorite tool. "Will this help?"

"A magnifying glass?" Ling asked as she held up the

tooth to look at it through the lens. "You really came prepared."

"Dev didn't come prepared for dinosaurs, Ling," Katie said. "She thinks she's a detective. Dev carries that thing around almost everywhere she goes because that's what Nancy Drew did."

Ling laughed.

"Would you please look at Katie's bones with my magnifying glass?"

"Sure," she said.

Ling turned the first piece over and over again, under the lens. She did the same with the second piece, without saying a word.

"Aren't Katie's bones talking to you?" I said.

Ling pursed her lips. "They're not saying much, girls. That's why getting them to a real museum is so important. There's all kinds of sophisticated imaging the museum paleontologists can do. I'm still just a student."

I sat back on my heels, more confused than ever about what Katie had found and whether Chip Donner—under the watchful eye of Steve Paulson—had switched out her bones for ordinary old sticks.

"I'll see you two later," Ling said. "I'm going to hang out with the other grad students for a while. I'm leaving the tooth in your care."

Katie and I knew what an honor that was, and that Ling would be close by so we really didn't have to worry about her special treasure. We changed into our pajamas and waited for Kyle to come back to the tent.

"Let's not tell Kyle about Chip Donner tonight," I said to Katie. "Ling's almost an expert and she couldn't even give us a clue about what's going on."

"I trust Kyle completely."

"I know you do. I just don't want to put him in a tough situation, between two groups of people he likes," I said. "It wouldn't be fair to him."

The flap of the tent rustled and I sat up with a start. "What's that?"

Kyle came through with water bottles and flashlights. "What did you think it was, Dev—a bear?"

I took a few deep breaths to calm down. "Katie's the one who's afraid of bears."

"You bet I am," she said.

"Let's level the playing field, Kyle," I said, reaching for water. "You've been to New York, cowboy. Did anything scare you there?"

Kyle lay down on top of his sleeping bag, one arm behind his head, and gave it a few moments' thought.

"Okay," he said. "Sure. I was pretty much afraid of

being underground, all closed in with no way to see the sky, riding on subway trains."

Katie laughed at him. "I can't believe it. You never told me that, Kyle. Dev and I ride the subway every day."

"Well, I didn't like it," he said. "How about you, Dev? What's got you spooked out here?"

"Truth?" I said. "You're not going to play another mean trick on me, are you?"

"No way."

"Snakes," I said, almost quivering as I spoke the word. "Katie's dad says there are rattlesnakes out here, all over the place."

"We got plenty of those," Kyle said with a mischievous grin. "I can wrangle one up for you if you like."

"You promised, Kyle. No games," I said, pulling my knees up to my chest. "So name something else that scared you in New York."

He thought for another few seconds. "Tall buildings. We don't have anything in Big Timber more than two stories high," he said. "Skyscrapers make me woozy."

"Like where Katie lives," I said, slapping my knees. "I can't believe it. What's scary about them?"

"Not her apartment exactly," Kyle said. "Great big ones, like the Empire State Building. The Cions took me up to the observation deck on the top, and I thought I was going to lose my lunch."

"That's so crazy," Katie said. "Dev and I could dance around the edge up there with our ballet slippers on. She and I used to take dance lessons together. Who knew heights like those made you nervous?"

"This is good for all of us," I said. "I mean, to talk this all out. My mom says it's okay to have fears of some things, as long as we know what they are and try to deal with them."

"Here we go," Katie said. "That's Dev's mother talking. Did I tell you, Kyle, that Dev's mom is the police commissioner of New York City? I mean, the entire city. And she's the first woman ever to hold that job."

I was the one blushing now, biting my lip. I was so fiercely proud of my mother, who had been appointed to that powerful position by the city's mayor.

"I mean, when we're home, Kyle," Katie said, "Dev acts like she's not afraid of anything. Nothing. That's because she's got the entire police force to back her up."

Kyle looked at me with all new respect. "That really rocks, Dev."

"Thanks, but I have nothing to do with it," I said. "It's all about my mother."

"What frightens you out here, Katie?" Kyle asked.

"Mountain lions, for sure."

"There are mountain lions on your property?" I asked. "When were you going to tell me that?"

"I spend so much time looking down in the tall grass so I can avoid rattlesnakes," she said, "that my father keeps reminding me that the big cats pounce on you from above, where they hide in the limbs of trees."

"You were right the first time, Kyle," I said. "These really are the Badlands."

"Not as bad as New York," he said. "I hate crowds, Dev. I hate all that pushing and shoving that people do to get where they want to go. I sort of worry that I'll be swept away with them and get lost."

"Don't worry about that, Kyle. You come back to New York and I'm betting Katie won't ever let you slip away in the crowd."

Katie tapped me on my head, which I had finally rested on my pillow.

"That's your whole list, Dev?" Kyle asked. "You bunking down for the night?"

"It's all I can think of for now."

"Then just be sure to shake out your moccasins in the morning, before you step into them," Kyle said.

"Why's that?" I said.

I looked down at the floor of the tent and almost

gagged. A gigantic black creature with a bunch of legs and a long tail was crawling into my moccasin. It was a scorpion, making himself at home in my shoe, and starting to move it across the carpet, like he was driving it away. I let out a scream that was loud enough to bring everyone running to our tent.

4

Kyle picked up my moccasin and calmly walked out through the flap to dispose of the venomous creature.

Steve Paulson followed Kyle back inside.

"I'm so sorry for bothering you, Steve," I said. "The scorpion kind of freaked me out."

"No problem at all, Dev. They come with the territory. Just be sure you close your eyes and start by counting sheep, like Mr. Cion has out back on the ranch," Steve said, turning to walk out. "Don't you conjure up visions of anything with eight arachnid legs or a tail that rattles when it's unhappy. Scorpions won't come after you. Just don't step on him or you'll feel that stinger. Better count sheep till you get drowsy."

I'd be counting for a very long time before I relaxed enough to fall asleep.

"This time tomorrow we'll be bunking in our own beds back at the house," Katie said. "My brother is great at squishing bugs."

"I'm concentrating on the dig," I said. Wilhelmina Ditchley had aimed to inspire confidence in her girls with every difficult experience. She'd never have let a scorpion set her back. "I want to find some fossils, too, and we've only got one day left."

"Kyle?" Katie said in her softest voice. "Maybe you and I can sit up for a while, over here on my sleeping bag, and keep a lookout for scorpions and stuff like that? Let Dev get plenty of rest for tomorrow."

That one really made me smile. I'd have to give Katie some lessons in subtlety when we got home. Did she really think she'd be making the tent safe for me by rubbing toes with Kyle Lowry?

I rolled over and slid down till my feet touched the bottom of my sleeping bag. The day's work in such intense heat had tired me out.

I was pretty determined not to leave Montana empty-handed, so I zoned out on Katie's chatter and set my thoughts on dinosaurs.

I was awakened by the noise of Ling rolling up her sleeping bag and gathering her belongings together.

"Good morning," I said to Ling and Katie as I pushed myself up and reached for my clothes. "What happened to Kyle? Did you talk him out of the tent last night?"

"Not funny," Katie said. "He actually prefers to sleep

out under the stars. It had nothing to do with me personally."

"You'll be so much smarter once you turn twelve next week. Wait and see," I said.

"If you two girls want to see something really spectacular, get ready as fast as you can," Ling said, "and we'll run down to the foot of the gulch and watch the sun come up over the ridge, before Steve and his team arrive. By the time they have their coffee at the campsite, they've missed the most beautiful part of the day."

"I'm game. C'mon, Katie."

"What about my bones?" she said, holding up the plastic box.

"They'll be perfectly fine right here," Ling said, "alongside my tooth. Even if you do get permission to keep them from the man who owns this land, you'd be doing a good thing if you let Steve have your fossils to study."

Katie placed her box on the ground. I could tell she was reluctant to leave it.

We went outside together to wash up and brush our teeth. Kyle was sitting on a log, looking out over the dig site while he waited for us.

"Here's an energy bar for each of you," Ling said, passing them out. "It's better than weighing ourselves down with bacon and eggs at the start of the day. We can grab something more later on. Ready to head down?"

"Sure," Kyle said. "I told Steve we'd be waiting for him at the bottom. We can't start till he gets here and gives us instructions for the day."

"Of course not," Ling said.

Kyle led us down a trail off to the side of the gulch. We wound our way down and around the scrub and sagebrush until we came to a clearing. The hillside looked even more daunting than it did the day before—higher and steeper, barren of all vegetation, and bound to be hotter once the sun reached its position overhead.

"Can you see the Crazies?" Ling asked.

"That's no way to talk about those nice people we're digging with," I said, laughing at her.

"Not unless you mean Chip Donner," Katie said.

Katie could hold a grudge, that's for sure. She was still edgy about the fact that Liza and I had solved a crime last month without her help.

"The Crazies aren't people," Ling said. "It's a mountain range—that one in the distance with snow on the peaks."

"The Crazy Mountains?" I asked. I looked off to the west, just where the ball of sunlight over my shoulder was dancing on the snowcapped points. "That's really what they're called?"

"They got their name when settlers were moving west through here, and the Native Americans—the Crows—used to ride up into the mountains because that's where they saw visions," Ling said. "Spiritual things."

"Badlands," Katie said, keeping her eye on Kyle, who had wandered off and headed up the slope. "The Crazies. Bear paw markings and snakeskins that have been shed. It all kind of makes me long for Manhattan. Piano lessons and homework don't seem so bad anymore."

Kyle was climbing fast now, probably higher than he should have been without Steve here to guide us.

Ling cupped her hands around her mouth and called out to him. "Better get back down, Kyle. Steve's in charge, you know."

He dropped to his knees on the brown sandstone. "You've got to see this, Ling! You're not going to believe it."

Ling bolted in Kyle's direction and I was only a few steps behind her. "You found something already?"

"Wait up!" Katie yelled.

"Grow those legs, Katie," I said. "You're moving slower than a brontosaurus."

"Oh, no!" Ling shouted, trying to keep up with Kyle as he got to his feet and veered off the hillside as though he was following a trail. "They're tire tracks. And they're right near where I found the tooth yesterday."

She pointed at the flame-colored orange circle she had spray-painted on the hill to mark her discovery.

Kyle Lowry was standing still. "Look at this, Ling. There's been a bulldozer here during the night. A small one, all right—like the size of a riding lawn mower—but big enough for someone to scoop something out of the bone bed with the bucket on the front of it."

"This is exactly where I was going to start digging today," she said, leaning over with her hands on her knees to catch her breath. "That was going to be *my* treasure to find."

"Hold on," I said. "Aren't you jumping the gun here? You don't have any proof that someone found fossils during the night. There's no evidence that something was taken out of the dirt, is there?"

"You may know a lot about evidence, Dev, but I've been on dozens of digs," Ling said. "This is what poachers *do*. They're trespassers. They sneak into digs sometimes in the middle of the night."

Kyle kicked at the dirt with the toe of his boot. "It's a big problem out west. Poachers trespass on private property when there are so many acres you can't watch over all of them, like on this ranch."

"For what?" I asked.

"Usually to hunt on your land, or fish your rivers and streams."

"In our work," Ling said, "the poachers come to steal the bones, once we've done all the hard work to find the fossils in the first place."

"On midget bulldozers?" I asked. "You'd think one of those would stand out like a sore thumb around here."

Kyle shook his head. "There are loads of them, Dev. There's a big mine not far from town, and the mini-dozers are used to go down into the mines and scoop up minerals."

"Don't worry, Ling," I said. "We can follow the tracks and figure out who sneaked in here while we were all asleep."

"Dev's really good at this kind of thing," Katie said. "I promise we'll all help find you some more dinosaur teeth."

"It's not teeth, Katie. It's much more than that," Ling said, discouragement dripping from her words.

"What then?" I asked.

"When you find several teeth, like our group did this week," she said, pointing at three other nearby orange circles on the ground, "Steve's right that there's a good chance there's a skull pretty close by. And the skull is the biggest prize of all, Dev."

"How come?"

"That's how fossil thieves work. Museums will pay a fortune for an intact dinosaur skull, complete with its jawbone. It's the easiest way to identify the species of the animal. We're all just picking up bits and pieces like we did yesterday, hoping the scientists will be able to put the puzzle together for us," Ling said, looking too close to tears for my taste. "Meanwhile, someone just sneaked in right under our noses and may have dug out the biggest treasure of all."

5

Kyle and I followed the tire tracks more than a hundred yards off to the right, while Katie brought up the rear.

The tracks ended when we reached a dirt road that ran parallel to the wide bone bed that we'd been digging on.

"What happened here?" I asked.

"Probably whoever was thinking about poaching something had a flatbed truck parked here," Kyle said. "It's how he brought the bulldozer and left with it."

The three of us were stumped. I turned to walk back to the spot where Ling was standing, guarding her piece of turf against all comers.

I pulled my cell phone out of my backpack.

"No reception here," Kyle said. "Don't you remember?"

"I know. I'm taking some pictures of the tracks."

Kyle shrugged and passed by me. "Just ordinary tracks."

"There's no such thing," I said, getting down on one

knee to snap a close-up of the indentations in the soil. "Every brand of tire has a unique tread mark."

"It's not that Dev is smarter than we are, Kyle," Katie said. "It's just that her mom finds out all these things in her job, and then Dev stores this useless information in her brain till the right moment when she can pluck it out to try to impress someone."

"You never know when stuff is going to come in handy," I said. "My mother has this amazing detective named Sam Cody who works with her. Sam once caught a major criminal because the guy was careless enough to drive on the grass in the middle of Central Park after fleeing the crime scene. There's a company that makes a business out of identifying every brand and model of treads on tires."

"That's neat," Kyle said.

"We could get lucky here."

Steve Paulson, Chip Donner, and the group of grad students and volunteers were making their way down from the ridge to start the day's work.

The three of us huddled with Ling.

"Did you find anything?" I asked her.

"How could you expect me to find something that's been taken away?"

"You don't know that for sure, do you? I mean, it's

possible the poacher didn't have any more productive a dig than I did yesterday."

She uncrossed her arms and pointed at a large hole in the dirt. "Don't you think something was scooped out of there, Dev? Isn't it obvious?"

"I'll admit that it looks like someone tried to lift out a big chunk of earth. But how would he—or she—know where to find the skull in all this dirt?"

Ling was rocking herself from side to side. "Maybe he was watching us all week."

"You mean you think it could be someone involved in Steve's project?" Katie asked.

I knew Katie was thinking of Chip Donner.

"Why not?" Ling said. "You know that two days before you got here, other people found teeth in that same area of the grid that I did. It's as good a guess as any."

"We've got to sound professional when we tell this to Steve," I said, trying to get the four of us to focus. "Let's start with the facts. Everyone in our group was accounted for last night, right? All sleeping in our tents."

"I wasn't in the tent," Kyle said. "But I didn't move from the spot once I got into my sleeping bag."

"You're not a suspect anyway," Katie said, smiling at Kyle.

I'd save it till later to tell Katie it was bad investigative form to take the pressure off Kyle before we even got started. How do we know what he did during the night?

"And Chip went home to sleep," Ling said. "He said his wife hadn't been feeling well all day and he wanted to be with her."

"Check," I said.

"I thought it was really a sweet thing," Ling said.

"We have to set a time frame for this," I said. "What time did you and the grad students go to sleep, Ling?"

"We were up till after one o'clock. I think it was one fifteen when I said good night to the others and came back to the tent."

"Did you see or hear anything going on down the slope?"

"Not then," Ling said. "A few of us even stood at the edge of the ridge and looked around, trying to imagine what it was like when all those terrible lizards—that's the Greek translation of the word 'dinosaurs'—roamed Montana. But there was nothing happening here at that hour."

"I'm surprised your Atwells didn't pick up anything, Dev," Katie said. "I didn't think they were ever off-duty."

"Sorry," Ling said. "What are your Atwells?"

"So, my grandmother's last name is Atwell," I explained, laughing. "Louella Atwell. And she has the most incredible hearing of anyone I've ever known. Like she could have heard my whisk broom brushing sand away from rocks if she'd been in a tent up above us yesterday."

"And Dev inherited that trait," Katie said. "She's got Atwell ears, and they've even helped her solve mysteries."

Kyle picked his head up and looked at me like I was an alien.

"Don't worry," I said. "I never heard a word that you and Katie were saying to each other last night. I promise. My ears fell asleep before I did."

There was no reason to let either of them know that the final thing Katie whispered to Kyle before I drifted off was that she was going to take a photograph of him at the Big Timber rodeo tonight to keep on her desk at home.

Me? I'd rather frame a picture of his good-looking pinto than his face.

"So, I'm guessing the poacher came in sometime between two in the morning and six," Kyle said.

"I suppose he knew exactly where to go," Ling said, "based on observing us the past couple of days, before you girls got here. Maybe the poacher took two or three practice scoops nearby, until he found what he was looking for. That's what we tell Steve."

"Hold your horses," I said. "Do you know how many times you've used the words 'guess' and 'suppose'? Real detectives don't go to work on the basis of guesses, okay? We have to reach our conclusions by reasoning, not by guessing. We have to be logical and factual."

"You're about to get Devlin Quick's lecture on Sherlock Holmes," Katie said.

"Have you ever read any of Sherlock's case studies?" I asked.

Both Ling and Kyle answered in the negative.

"He's the greatest detective who ever lived."

"He didn't *live*, Dev. He's a character in a bunch of books and stories."

"The thing about good books, Katie, is that if they are really well-told tales, the characters come alive. They're better companions than a lot of people I've met."

"What's up with you kids?" Steve Paulson called out from the trail next to the bone bed. "What's going on up there?"

"Let me take the lead on this one, if you don't mind," I said. "Let's make deductions, so we sound intelligent, okay? And while we're at it, let's all use our keenest powers of observation to watch how all the others react to the news that we've been visited by a poacher. That's what made Sherlock brilliant. He was a careful observer of other people."

"So you admit there's been a poacher, Dev?" Ling asked.

"The tire track evidence and the scoops in the earth support the fact that there was a trespasser, for sure. What you're guessing at is whether anyone actually found what he was looking for and got away with your treasure," I said. "Let's give it a fair shot and get on with our dig for the time being. We're not even sure who we're looking for or what, if anything, they took."

I turned away from our little group and started to jog down the incline toward Steve. Rope lines had been set up on the hill to mark the outer boundaries of the dig. I didn't want to disturb any of the previous finds, so I ducked under one of the lines and headed down on the scraggly trail just south of the tire tracks.

Steve was waving his arms over his head. "No, Dev, no! Stop running!"

He sounded frantic as he tried to slow me down.

"It's okay, Steve. I'll explain everything to you," I said, picking up speed like a boulder rolling down the side of a slope.

"You've got to stop, Dev!"

I wanted to please him, of course, but I wanted him to hear the story from me.

I didn't understand why he wanted to stop me until it was too late.

My feet were pounding into the dirt and my arms were pumping back and forth. I was eager to give Steve the news about the trespasser and to start to put my clues together. I was closing in on him, with Katie and Kyle somewhere in the distance behind me.

I kept on running toward Steve until suddenly, the earth gave way beneath my legs.

Before I could even blink, I was up to my knees in quicksand.

6

"Stop wiggling, Dev," Chip Donner said, barking at me with his gruff voice. "I've got you and I'm not going to let go."

I was sinking deeper into the pile of soaking wet goo that was hidden beneath the dry brown dirt. Chip Donner had lay down on the solid ground next to my hole and stretched out his long arm to grab my elbow with his powerful right hand.

"Stay still or you'll make it worse, Dev," Katie yelled to me. "Please don't squirm."

"I'm not sq—"

"No talking, Dev," Chip said. "Steve's got the rope from the boundary line, and we'll wrap that around you and pull you out. You're going to be okay."

I bit my lip and tried to keep myself from turning my head to look for Steve. I was a strong swimmer—a freestyler on the Ditchley swim team. My instinct was to kick my legs like I was treading water. But I knew this was not as friendly a spot as a swimming pool.

"I can't watch this," Katie said, putting both hands over her eyes.

Chip's fingers were digging into my skinny arms. It was nothing for me to complain about since his hands were all that separated me from something worse that I didn't want to think about.

"Okay, now, Dev," Chip said. "Steve and Kyle are right behind you. Kyle throws a lasso better than anyone in Sweet Grass County. It's going to drop right onto your shoulders, and we'll get it under your arms and yank you out. You good with that?"

I nodded my head up and down.

I could tell by the dazed look on Katie's face, staring over the top of my head, that Kyle was directly behind me, ready to throw his lasso.

"Here it comes, Dev," Steve called out.

The loop of rope landed on me like dead weight. I felt myself drop down another inch.

"Raise both hands as high as you can," Chip said. "One at a time. Go on, I'll grab your other arm when you lift this one."

With my free arm, I reached for the sky, letting the rope slip down into the mud, below my waist. Chip grabbed for that elbow and got me on the second try, telling me to raise the one he'd been holding on to as fast as I could.

Kyle tightened up on the rope and I felt my whole body jerk backward.

"Hand it over," Steve said to Kyle. "You hang on, Dev. I may bounce you a bit."

Steve yanked me out of the hole and onto dry ground in less than a minute. Katie was the first one to reach my side, hugging me like she thought she'd never see me again.

I was trembling all over, trying to make light of the situation but not doing that well enough to fool anyone.

"I thought quicksand was only a feature in bad movies," I said. "Careful, Katie. I'm not even sure this stuff will come off in a bubble bath."

"You hit a mudflat, Dev," Steve said, trying to calm me and everyone else around. "You were sunk in about as deep as you could go, so there wasn't much more to fear. No worries there. Just an old-fashioned mudflat."

"What's that?" Easy for him to say I shouldn't have been so scared at this point.

"They happen occasionally where the surface looks just like the rest of the soil we've been walking on. But since this used to be swampland and marsh once upon a time when this part of Montana was an inland sea, we stumble on these underground pockets of mud every now and then," Steve said. "You feeling okay?"

"Better now," I said. "I felt like I was falling through to the center of the Earth."

"Nah. We wouldn't have let you go very far. It's why I was trying to steer you off that side trail, though. We've never tested anything except the ground that's within the rope lines, and the path we use off to the other side to come down in the mornings."

"Thank goodness for those rope lines," I said as Steve helped me onto my feet. "Hey, Kyle, I owe you for that perfect toss."

He was too modest to accept my thanks. "Easier to get hold of you while you're standing still, stuck in a mudflat, than to lasso a bucking bronco. Good practice for the rodeo, Dev."

"Great deduction you made there," Katie said, testing to make sure that my sense of humor had come out of the mud intact. "You're no Sherlock, Dev. Why don't you just tell Steve why you were running?"

"Can it wait till we get you some clean clothes and take you over to the river to wash up?" Steve asked.

"It's pretty important," I said.

"Maybe it's not something everybody around us

needs to hear about," Chip said, gesturing to the group of volunteer diggers who had gathered near the foot of the incline to see what was causing the excitement.

"I'm not one to be rude, Chip, but maybe that's exactly what it is," I said. "The four of us got down here early this morning, just to check out the sunrise and the scenery. But it was pretty quickly obvious to all of us that there was someone trespassing on the bone bed last night."

"Trespassing?" Steve asked. His brow furrowed and his whole body seemed to tense when he repeated the word.

Chip held his forefinger up to his mouth and said, "Shhhh."

"There were tire tracks on the hillside, Steve," I said.

"And some scoops in the earth, right near the place that I found the tooth yesterday," Ling added.

The two men looked at each other without speaking. I couldn't read the expressions on their faces, but they seemed more concerned about news of trespassers than they did about what I feared was going to be my journey to the center of the Earth.

Chip had kept me from sinking deeper into the mudflat by holding on to me, and I was thankful for his kindness. I didn't want to harbor any unfounded suspicions about him, to add to Katie's hunch, so I was trying to keep a level head.

"Have you got extra clothes in the tent?" Steve asked.

"Nothing clean, sir."

"My things will be a little big on Dev," Ling said, "but I've got jeans and some shirts that I can spare."

"Let's let you wash up, little lady," Chip said. "We've got hours to sort this out."

"But it's our last day," Katie said. "What if poachers came in last night? What if they took something valuable?"

"I'll be sure to tell that to the sheriff when I call," Steve said. "Look, Katie, what's more important to you? Your best friend is shaking like a leaf on a cottonwood tree, and you're worried about some tracks in the sand?"

"I'm really going to be fine, Steve," I said, forcing a smile.

Steve was rattled, that's for sure. He didn't want to let on to us how much he was, but calling the sheriff must be a big deal in these parts. Then again, someone trespassing on a dig site was even more worrisome.

"What you need to do, if you don't mind, is convince Katie not to tell her mother about this—um, this misstep of mine, Steve," I said, "so that Mrs. Cion doesn't feel the need to tell *my* mom."

"What's there to tell? Everybody's doing fine," Chip Donner said, brushing the dirt off his clothes. "Best of all, you get to keep on digging. I'm hoping it's going to be somebody's lucky day."

I waited with Katie and Chip while Ling ran back up to the ridge to get me a change of clothes. Steve had drawn the group into a circle to give instructions for the day's work, so we stayed quiet until he finished and set them off up the hill.

"You must get used to poachers in your business," I said to Chip, "but I'd find them really annoying."

"Back home we'd call them thieves," Katie said, "and Dev's mother would catch them. Fast. That's why her nickname is Commissioner Quick."

Katie was trying to keep things light, but I'd heard that joke about my mom's name too many times to laugh at it again. She had rolled her finger in the mud on my pants leg and was writing her initials on my forearm.

"You have to steal something to be a thief," Chip said.

Steve joined our conversation. "Could be, Katie, that it was just a diversion someone tried to cause."

"What do you mean by that?" she asked.

"Might be someone jealous of the operation we're

running over here. Took a run in during the night just to snoop around and see what we're doing."

"That sounds pretty weak to me, sir, if you don't mind my opinion," I said.

Maybe it wasn't my place to butt in, but Steve's whole manner had changed since we told him about the tire tracks. He wasn't so cheerful now. He was trying to downplay the trespass. But it sounded like a real problem to me.

"Seems more like somebody was scooping around than snooping," Katie said.

"Okay, I'll even give the trespassers a few scoops. They're trying to divert my attention from the real job at hand," Steve said. "Take my focus away from keeping this team together."

"That's really interesting," I said. "A diversionary tactic which throws us all off our game. You're saying we could be wasting this entire day if you panicked and made us stop to hunt down the trespassers."

"Time is really precious to us out here," Steve said. "There are only so many weeks before the seasons change and then the harsh weather and shorter daylight hours cut us off."

"Sometimes, Dev, it's just a local rancher who's curious about how we do what we're doing," Chip said. "I've run into guys on neighboring property who'd like to try to dig up their own bones and sell them off before we can. Just harmless folks who live around here and hope to win the lottery by finding a dinosaur leg by copycatting what we do."

Steve seemed to have one idea and Chip quite another. Steve thought the trespassers were intending to throw him off course, while Chip chalked it up to nosy neighbors. I had to wonder whether they were being honest with us, or just trying to keep us from getting spooked. What if these nighttime invaders were really criminals, looking to make off with valuable fossils?

"How about we give you and Ling some privacy down at the edge of the river, so you can wash that muck off and get back to digging?" Steve asked.

"I'd like that," I said.

"I'll go with you," Katie said.

"I'd rather get you started up on the hill, Katie." Steve looked like he'd spent enough time with us kids because of the trouble I'd caused—or because of the news about the trespassers. He was ready to work, and probably to alert the sheriff. "Dev can catch up to you."

"But—"

"It's okay, Katie," I said. "I'll come right back after I change my clothes."

Steve uncrossed his arms and pointed at the incline, just to the right of the orange spray-painted circle where Ling had found her tooth yesterday, and about ten feet below where the tire tracks had entered the property during the night.

"Pick up your tools, Katie," Steve said. He was dead serious now. "Let's see if you can earn your keep again today."

7

By the time I took my muddy things off and dipped into the chilly river water, dried myself, and dressed in Ling's clothes, we got back to find Katie on her hands and knees, using a small ice pick to chip away at the rocks she encountered on her slow climb.

I dropped down next to her after Ling walked off to join the older students, and Katie paused to ask me how I was doing. "I'm fine, I think."

"You're still shaking, Dev."

"That water is really cold."

"You can't fool me," Katie said. "I know you better than that."

I picked up a small shovel—like a garden tool—and leaned over to start to dig. "Back to work," I said. "I don't want to go home empty-handed."

"I sort of don't want to go home at all yet."

"Kyle fever, huh?"

Katie got back on all fours with her tool in hand, and we inched our way upward side by side. Pretty soon, we were both sweating so much that the coolness of the mud and the nippy river were a distant memory.

We poked around for more than an hour before Steve called out for the first mid-morning break. Kyle was passing bottles of water to all the volunteers.

I stood up and walked over to Steve's position, where the graduate students had gathered around him.

"We're off to a good start today," Steve said. "Ling found two more teeth, not far from yesterday's discovery—"

"Why is it always Ling?" Katie asked me.

"Hey, you found some little bones. There's no room for jealousy in a bone bed."

"Can you look at these?" Steve said, holding out his hand for all of us to see. "These are duckbill dino teeth, for certain."

"How can you tell?" Katie asked.

"Good question. As I was saying last night, teeth give us a lot of information." Steve held up one of the fossils between his thumb and forefinger. "Meat-eaters—carnosaurs—have sharper teeth."

We all nodded.

"Duckbills ate berries and plants, like honeysuckle and evergreens," he said.

"Excuse me," Katie said, "but how do you even know what kind of plants there were so many millions of years ago."

Steve grimaced at the second interruption. He didn't know, I guess, that at Ditchley we're taught to ask questions about everything we don't understand. Katie was a pro at that.

"The rock formations that were created way back then actually have remains of pollen in them, Katie. Pollen that botanists have matched to berry bushes and dogwood trees."

"Pretty cool," she said, no doubt thinking of more things to ask to keep her off her hands and knees.

"Back to duckbills," Steve said. "Not very many reptiles chew their food. They can bite and chop and swallow, but they don't chew. Duckbills had scores of teeth—in rows, actually, on both sides of their jaws. They were grinders, which was the perfect apparatus for processing plant food. They were very successful dinosaurs."

"Why are they called 'duckbills'?" Katie asked.

One of the grad students, impatient to move on, answered her question. "Check them out, next time you go to a natural history museum, Katie. They've got really distinctive skull shapes, these dinos. They're really broad and very flat, so they form kind of a beak. Just like a duck."

"Don't forget about the crests," Ling said. "Some of the duckbills have crests, just like their feathered counterparts. And webbed feet, too."

"Super-ducks!" Katie shouted. "That's what I'd call them. Let's go find us one."

Her voice carried over the whole hillside. The older volunteers, scattered around the incline, turned to see why Katie was yelling at top volume.

Steve Paulson was going to think twice about us kid volunteers from now on—that was clear from the expression on his face. "Go for it, Katie. And remember, so far these seem to be the fossils of juvenile duckbills."

"Is that unusual?" I asked.

"Juveniles?" Steve seemed to be relaxed when I spoke. Maybe he was relieved that I was participating again, after my misstep. "They're the rarest of all fossil finds. People have been finding dinosaur bones for centuries, thinking—back in the old days—that they were the remains of giants. But it was in 1824, in England, that the first scientific connection was made to an ancient animal."

He went on. "It was another one hundred years before any babies were identified, in Mongolia. They're still pretty hard to come by. So this is an exciting day for us, and I want you all to get back to work with renewed enthusiasm."

Katie beat me back to our spot on the hill and got right to work. We scraped and dug and whisked off pieces of rock with our little brooms. When lunchtime came, we trudged off to the side and tried to shade ourselves behind a scrubby bush.

"Back to work," Katie said. "Four hours to go."

"I've got pebbles digging into my kneecaps," I said. "They'll be black and blue for sure."

"Look who's complaining today? Pouting about pebbles. Really, Dev?"

"The only things I've found since we started are a scorpion in my shoe and a mudflat!"

Every now and then, when I scanned the group above and below us, I could see Steve and Chip examining objects the others were holding out to them—finds that these volunteers had made.

Ling was about twenty feet above Katie and me. She walked down to grab another bottle of water and stopped to talk to us.

"How are you two doing?" she asked.

"Fine, thank you," Katie said, hunching over her dig site as though protecting it from a poacher.

"See what's going on there?" she said, pointing to a place in the soil—a dip in the earth—where the red mudstone met up with a patch of green mudstone. "Want some help?"

"I'll call you if I need advice," Katie said, offering a smile to Ling.

"Okay, then." She walked on, but kept looking back over her shoulder.

"Do you know what she was talking about?" Katie asked me.

"Not a clue. You should have let her help you," I said, scraping the pebbles off my knees.

"C'mon, Dev. Don't you value your independence?"

"Of course I do, but—"

"You've got to see this," Katie said, straightening her back and reapplying herself to the dirt in front of her. "It's like a hollow bowl here, once you scratch the surface. It's bigger than our kitchen sink."

When I picked my head up, I could see Katie digging furiously with both hands, like a dog pawing into the ground to find a hidden bone.

"Slow down," I said, swiveling around so I could dig, too.

But Katie was clearing the soil away from the top and sides of the bowl all by herself. The next thing I knew, she had uncovered seven or eight little mounds—black ones, spotted with gray, that were sort of planted within the dirt bowl. They stuck out of the concave hollowed-out spot in the ground like a bunch of upside-down cardboard coffee containers.

Ling must have overheard us. She was running back to Katie, leaning in over her shoulder. Her jaw dropped before she gathered herself to speak. "Don't touch them. Let's get Steve or Chip over here."

She turned and called out their names, waving her arms over her head.

"I can't believe you made this amazing discovery. I wish it had been me," Ling said.

"What are they?" I asked.

"They're eggs. They're unhatched dinosaur eggs," she said. "Katie, you've found an entire clutch."

Ling was trying to get Steve's attention.

"I don't even know what a clutch is," Katie said.

"It's what you call all of the eggs that a reptile lays in one grouping," I said.

"Do I really have a clutch of super-duckbills?" Katie said, taking her whisk broom from her jeans pocket and throwing it up in the air like it was a baton.

"It's incredible," I said, hugging my friend from behind. "You bet you do. You have the super-find of the entire dig!"

8

Steve was on his knees, gazing in wonder at Katie's find. She was glued to the dirt, right beside him, refusing to move away from her triumphant discovery.

Chip was commanding all the volunteers to keep their positions, but allowing Kyle and the grad students to circle in around the bowl to examine Katie's eggs.

We were all snapping cell phone shots of the unusual sight. The whole crater looked like a miniature version of how I imagined the surface of the moon to be—gray and black, craggy and uneven, with worn markings that seemed as old as time.

Chip sprayed an enormous neon circle of paint to mark the spot, and we all gathered around inside it.

"You get to name that, Katie," Steve said. "Anything you want."

Katie looked at me and laughed. "It's got to be the Ditch, Steve. For Ditchley. That's the nickname of the school Dev and I go to, and it's the perfect name for a clutch that was hiding in a scooped out hole in the earth."

"I'm good with that."

"Do I get to name the mama, too? The super-duck who laid the eggs?"

"Why not?" Steve said. "We may find some traces of her, even after you two are gone."

"Then she's going to be Willie D," Katie said. "For Wilhelmina Ditchley. If Ms. Ditchley were still alive, she'd be so proud of me, don't you think, Dev?"

"For certain."

"I don't even care if poachers made off with anything last night," Katie said, leaning back to whisper to me. "I've got the best buried treasure of all."

"You're off the charts, Katie," I said, patting her on the shoulder.

"How do I get my clutch out of here, Steve?" she asked. "I've got to take one of these eggs to my science class in the fall."

"Not so fast, missy," Steve said.

"But they're mine, aren't they?" Katie said, talking faster than she could think. "At least I sure hope they will be once we talk to the ranch owner and he agrees to let me keep them."

"Think bigger picture, Katie," I said. "This isn't about *you*. These eggs might belong in a museum, not on your mom's kitchen counter."

I stood up and continued to brush pebbles off my knees. "Sorry, but these stones really hurt."

"They're not pebbles digging into you," Ling said, reaching down to pick up some of the debris. "They're fragments of fossils. Place them onto some matting for me, will you, so we can preserve them and pack them up with the rest of the find?"

"Eleven eggs," Katie said. "I'm counting eleven of them. Can't I have just one?"

"Use your common sense, girl," Chip shouted out.

Steve held his arm out to his side to calm the other man. "It's quite difficult to extract this entire nest from the ground, in one piece, without disturbing—"

"Extract the Ditch," Katie said, laughing at the whole idea of it. "You meant to say you have to dig out this whole Ditch. It's got a name now, you guys."

"Okay. What we'll have to do starting tomorrow is—"

"But Dev and I won't be here tomorrow."

"We'll let you know every little step we take, Katie," Steve said. "Look closely and you'll see that the ends of the eggs are embedded in the soil. You can't lift any one of them out separately. Remember, they're petrified, just like other fossils."

"Yeah," Katie said. "I get it."

"There's a delicate process for lifting this entire

nest—the Ditch—out of the ground safely," Steve said.

"How do you do it?" I asked.

"Do you know what plaster of Paris is?" Steve asked.

"Sure," I said.

"You do?" Katie asked. "How do you know?"

"Booker's mom's an orthopedic surgeon. Remember?" I said. "Those doctors use plaster of Paris—it's a kind of powder that they mix with water—to make casts when you have broken bones."

"We use the same technique to make plaster molds, girls," Steve said. "Chip and I will soak some burlap strips in wet plaster, and then wrap the entire Ditch—eggs and all—and cover it in a cast so it doesn't break apart, to get it safely back to the museum in Manhattan."

I was staring at the large hole in the earth, and its eleven mounds of buried treasure, sticking up in the air every which way—duckbill eggs. "But first you've got to get that whole thing out of the ground, Steve, before you make a cast for it. How do you do that?"

"We'll have to get a bulldozer in here," he said, "with a large scoop on the end of it."

"Just like the poachers used last night," I said, grimacing at the thought of what those people might have done if they'd come across Katie's Ditch.

"Trespassers, maybe. But you've got no reason to call them poachers," Steve said. "Look at this incredible treasure trove that they missed. Sort of goes to show they weren't trying very hard to find anything. Not half as hard as Katie."

I was happy for my best friend, trying to force back down into my throat that little bit of envy that was bubbling up. *You can't envy your friends,* my grandmother Lulu liked to tell me, *or you won't have them for very long. Delight in their good fortune.* Lulu's advice was usually spot-on.

"You let us get your nest back to the museum in New York, ask the scientists to tell us exactly what we've got and how rare it is, and then you and I can talk again about what you want to do with these things," Steve said to Katie.

I didn't think anyone would hear me talking to Kyle. "Will you do me a favor?"

He nodded. Kyle was the silent type, which served him well in this kind of situation.

"Get me some photos of the tire treads of that bulldozer when the crew brings it in tomorrow and e-mail them to me when you get back home," I said. My mother would know an expert who could compare the two sets of tire tracks—the ones I took today and the ones on the bulldozer. Maybe that will be a useful clue.

Kyle smiled and gave me a thumbs-up.

"That's fine with me, Steve," Katie said. "In fact, I guess I sounded kind of selfish, asking to take one of the eggs for myself."

"Well, you were just excited, and I understand that."

"I'd actually like *three* of the eggs, not just one. I'll wait for them, but I'd like Kyle and Dev each to have one also."

"Ixnay on an egg for me, Katie," I said. "I'd rather think of them all on display in the museum where thousands of people could see how cool they are."

"I could come visit them, too," Kyle said. "Dev's right."

Katie got to her feet. "I can see the plaque under the glass case already. 'KATIE CION: THE DISCOVERER OF WILLIE D. AND THE DITCH.'"

"Yeah, except no one's found Willie yet," I said. "Don't let your imagination run away with you."

"Who's getting back to work?" Chip called out to all the older kids.

"Katie, you can stay right here with me for the rest of the day," Steve said. "Let's dig around the Ditch and see if we can come up with anything related to your clutch."

"Kyle and Dev, too?"

"Sure thing."

We were all on our knees, back to the grunt work with our picks and our whisk brooms. But I was tingling with excitement now as Steve reminded us how rare Katie's find was.

"You never know, Katie," Steve said. "Every paleontologist who goes on a dig hopes to find fossils—something unusual, something rare. And the really big prize is the discovery of a new species."

"You mean there are still species of dinosaurs that haven't been found yet?" Kyle asked.

"You can count on that," Steve said. "Fifty years ago, people—even professionals in my field—thought that dinos were cold-blooded animals, slow and stupid."

Everywhere I put my little spade, all I came up with was dirt. There wasn't going to be a Eureka! moment for me.

"Now many of us believe they were warm-blooded, smarter than we'd thought, and really able to run fast. We never imagined they traveled in herds—which they did—and certainly not that they nested in colonies. But recent digs have confirmed those things."

Katie was staring at her clutch with great pride, and I couldn't blame her.

"It's okay, Katie," Steve said. "You can touch your eggs. You won't break them if you just rub the top."

She leaned in and stroked the rough exterior of two of the eggs.

"I guess I never thought of reptiles as laying eggs," Kyle said. "Rattlesnakes don't."

"Rattlers are ovoviviparous," Steve said. "There are eggs, but they hatch inside the mother's body."

"Ovoviviparous," Katie said. "What a really cool word that is."

"Could we just not talk about rattlesnakes?" I asked. "At least not till Katie and I get on the plane tomorrow."

"But plenty of reptiles do lay eggs, Katie," Steve said. "Turtles and crocodiles. They're oviparous."

"I like the other way better. I like saying ovoviviparous," Katie said.

"If you can repeat it quickly, five times in a row, you might be able to be a paleontologist," Steve said to her.

"So even though your fossils are millions and millions of years old," I said, "you're still learning new things about them?"

"We are, Dev."

"Our science teacher told us that birds are living dinosaurs," I said. "Like they both came from a common ancestor."

"That's the latest debate in the world of paleontology," Steve said. "We're all out in the field, looking for fossils to fill in the gaps in our knowledge of these creatures. Laying eggs is an example of a trait that birds and dinosaurs share, just as caring for their young in a nest is. One of the great things about science is that in most fields, it's still evolving. We learn new things all the time."

"So you might find entire duckbill fossils right here?" I asked.

"We're hoping," Steve said. "Might even get lucky one day and find some fossils with crests."

"Crests?" I asked. "What would that tell you?"

"You know how ducks—and some other birds, like parrots and cockatoos—have crests on top of their heads?"

"Sure. I've seen them at the zoo."

"The earliest duckbill fossils found in Montana had no crests—no bony structure poking up a bit above their eyes," Steve said. "Then, just a few years ago at another dig not far from here, one of my colleagues found some crested skulls."

"I get it. That might give you more proof that dinos do have some of the same ancestors as birds."

"That's the notion. But you can't push these theories

if you're a scientist, Dev. The evidence has to come to you."

Katie was stretched out full-length on the dirt, running her fingers over her eggs. "I wish I could stay out here and keep digging," she said. "Wouldn't you love to discover an entirely new species, Dev?"

"That would be epic," I said.

"We could call the species the Cion-o-saurus," she said, grinning. "*Cionosaurus katus.* Beast of the Badlands."

9

I was sorry to leave the site of the dig that afternoon. We packed up our gear and one of the volunteers drove us back to Big Timber.

This was my first trip out west. Each time we drove along the highway, since I had arrived, I was pretty amazed by the wide open spaces that spread out on both sides of the road. You could go for miles without seeing any houses, and then there would be farms with large barns and animals like cattle and sheep grazing along the fences that bordered the property.

There were also wild animals everywhere you could look—and not the scary kind. I especially liked the pronghorn antelopes and the huge elk that sometimes showed themselves when the sun started to go down.

Back at the Cion ranch, Katie's mom greeted us. We told her all about what Katie found and she assured us that her husband would call and ask the ranch owner if Katie could keep the bones when Steve finished his research.

We showered and changed our clothes and headed

back into town to go to the Sweet Grass County Rodeo for our last night in Montana.

There were a lot of contests, so we settled into our seats in the stands and got ready to cheer on the bull riders and pony racers.

The best event of the evening was the one featuring bucking broncos. It was best, of course, because we had a friend to root for.

When his turn was announced, Kyle's bronco burst out of the pen and into the ring of the small stadium like someone had lit a fire under his tail. The horse was bucking from the moment he hit the ground, kicking up a dust storm and jumping from side to side to throw his rider off his back.

Katie's hands were clasped in front of her mouth, which had the benefit of stopping the squealing she'd been doing when the event began.

Kyle was concentrating on staying on the horse. His right hand gripped the reins while his left arm was swinging in the air, helping to balance him as he got rocked around.

The announcer counted the time until the horse bucked Kyle onto the ground. A rider had to make the eight second mark for a score to count in our age group. It wasn't a pretty sight, but nine and a half seconds in the saddle was good enough to win Kyle first prize in the junior division.

Watching the action at the rodeo and enjoying the barbecue there was a perfect ending to our time in Big Timber. It was dusk, and I was pretty worn out after the excitement of the day.

Katie and Kyle walked off together to buy ice-cream sandwiches for us, while I sat with Katie's mom in the grandstand.

"Are you okay, Dev?" she asked.

"Yes, Mrs. Cion. It's been a great vacation. I can't thank you enough for including me in it."

"Katie wouldn't have come without you. Now she's going home, all full of herself with her great big discovery, and Kyle's got a blue ribbon tonight," Mrs. Cion said. "Can't we win a prize for you somehow? Are you feeling disappointed, Dev?"

"Not at all! I'm good. Katie and I have had so much fun out here."

"We'd better be getting back to the ranch," she said. "We've got a long travel day tomorrow."

I knew Katie wasn't going to want to say good-bye to Kyle. Dressed in his chaps and boots and ten-gallon hat, he looked like an authentic rodeo champion.

"I've been thinking about Katie's birthday next

week," I said, "and I may have figured out exactly what she wants."

Mrs. Cion smiled at me. "So you've been getting hints, too? Something about a locket she can wear every day?"

"Oh, no. Nothing like that," I said, shaking my head. "Nothing like jewelry."

"That would be a healthy change, Dev. What has Katie told you?"

It wasn't exactly anything that Katie had said, but it suddenly occurred to me that a night at the museum would be the perfect birthday celebration. I'd been there myself for another party, and I was pretty sure Katie would like the idea.

"Well, she's so pumped up by our two days on the dig and the fact that her nest and baby bones are being shipped to the museum to be examined, that she really wants to have a sleepover party—you know, a small one—at the museum."

"Devlin Quick," Mrs. Cion said, turning to me and raising an eyebrow. "Are you sure about this?"

"Absolutely certain."

I never lied. I knew better than to do that. But a fib-let was an entirely different thing. Fiblets always contained a large kernel of truth, to which I added a bit of wishful thinking. Nothing dishonest at all.

"Does the museum let you do that?"

"Yes, ma'am. One of the girls on the swim team had her party there this spring," I said. "I think there were eight of us and a chaperone—her mom, of course. Everybody in sleeping bags, which really makes it fun. And you have to pay the museum something, but that's like making a contribution to a great cause, isn't it? So educational and all that."

"What a great idea. I'll make a call before we leave for the airport tomorrow and see if I'm not too late to book a slumber party there next weekend," Mrs. Cion said. "We can always get Katie a locket for Christmas."

By Christmas, Katie would be so over Kyle that she'd be thanking me for arranging such a good caper.

With a little luck, Steve will have shipped the fossils back to New York by then, and Ling will be in residence to give us a private tour of the lab where the bones will be examined.

We could even use the opportunity to try to check to see if anyone had switched Katie's little bones on her that first night at the dig, for sure. Maybe it would be our chance to talk with Ling about that, if she was there.

Katie and Kyle were laughing as they walked back toward us.

"You'll help me with the guest list, won't you, Dev?"

"Absolutely. She'll want some of the girls from school, and if it's okay with you to have a guy, we'd want to invite Booker Dibble for sure. He loves dinosaurs, too."

"That would be terrific, Dev. We adore Booker, but—"

"It's okay, Mrs. Cion. They make you have a chaperone for your group."

"Then it's all good," she said. "I'm so glad Katie confided in you."

"Well, sometimes you just know someone so well you can figure out what they're thinking," I said. "Even if they don't exactly say the words out loud."

Katie would definitely want that party if she knew how much it meant to me to get us inside the most dino-smart place in the world.

"I'll even make cupcakes for Katie," I said.

"It's beginning to sound like a plan. Shall we keep it a secret?" Mrs. Cion said.

"Yes," I said. "Top secret."

"Then let's start talking about the contest, 'cause here they come."

Mrs. Cion waved and reached her hand out to take the ice cream that Kyle and Katie had carried back for us as she and Kyle climbed back up onto the grandstand.

"What are you two giggling about?" Katie asked.

The announcer was declaring the winner of the mutton-busting contest. The entrants were five- and six-year-old kids riding on sheep like Kyle had done with the bronco.

"Have you seen these mutton-busters, Katie?" I asked. "They're the cutest things I've ever watched."

"Kyle did that when he was a little kid," Katie said. "Didn't you, Kyle?"

"Yeah. My mom's got pictures of me hanging on to one of our sheep for dear life, back when I was four years old."

"Can I have one of those pictures?" Katie asked.

There she goes, I thought to myself, with that silly idea for her locket. She'd be much better off with a behind-the-scenes tour of the museum than some goofy shot of Kyle sitting on a load of mutton.

"Guess so."

Katie clasped her hands together and did her happy dance, which always made me laugh.

"Here's what I think," Katie said, leaning in to talk to her mother and me. "That I am the luckiest girl in the world right now."

I was licking the vanilla ice cream that was dripping from the edges of the sandwich. "I'll say."

"A week out here with my mom and my best friend,

lots of time with Kyle—who helped save Dev's life today—"

"What?" Mrs. Cion said, all the color draining out of her face. "What do you mean? What happened?"

"She's just kidding, Mrs. Cion," I said, trying to downplay my accident so as not to upset Katie's mother—or my own. "I slipped and fell on my tail when I was running down the hill this morning. Kyle gave me a hand to get me back on my feet. Saved me from embarrassing myself."

Katie blushed, realizing her mistake. "That's what I meant, Mom. Dev's just fine."

Mrs. Cion looked me over from head to toe.

"I was saying all the good things that were going on this week," Katie continued, playfully puffing her chest to sound like a grown-up as she went on. "I wasn't finished. I found a clutch of unhatched dino eggs, which may advance scientific knowledge in the field of paleontology for decades—"

"Get a grip on yourself, Katie Cion," her mother said. "Stop boasting."

"Those were Steve's words, Mom. I'm just repeating what he told us."

"That's a direct quote, ma'am," Kyle said.

"I just mean, Mom, that I'm so happy that Dad

encouraged me and Dev and Kyle to go on this dinosaur dig," Katie said. "I almost didn't do it."

"You are so very lucky," I said, "and I got to tag along with you, too. I'll thank your dad when we get back to New York, for sure."

I knew Katie was grateful for her good luck. It was her dad who had the idea that Katie would have fun on the dig, and he included me in the trip. I liked her dad a lot, which made me think of my own father, who had been killed before I was born. I knew how lucky Katie was.

10

The flight from Bozeman, Montana, back to New York was five hours long. It seemed like forever.

Mrs. Cion sat across the aisle from us, with Katie squeezed between a stranger and me—I had the window seat.

"What are you reading?" she asked me. We hadn't talked much since we left the rodeo. I was sad—my own doing, with my thoughts about my father—and really exhausted.

"*Treasure Island*."

"Is that on our summer reading list?" Katie said, still buzzing from her time with Kyle. "I haven't even glanced at that yet. Is that why you're reading it? I thought it was a boys' book."

"I'm reading it because I love Robert Louis Stevenson," I said. "My mother used to put me to sleep reciting his poems to me at night when I was a little kid."

Stevenson's verses always soothed me when I was worried about having nightmares. He wrote about garden swings, lamplighters, the pleasant land of counterpane, and my favorite of all about his shadow.

"Besides, Katie," I said, "there's no such thing as boys' books or girls' books. They're either good or bad, the way I look at it. This one is all about buried treasure, just like the fossils we were looking for."

I put my nose back in my book.

"Dev," Katie said, interrupting me, "can we talk for a few minutes?"

I put my finger in the page of the book where Katie stopped me. "Sure."

"Then don't look out the window when I've got something to say to you."

"Don't be so bossy."

"Wow, you're grouchy today, Dev."

"Sorry."

I didn't know one Great Lake from another, but looking down from 35,000 feet in the air, unable to see the shore on the far side of the vast body of water we were flying over, this one looked as wide as the ocean. I stared for a few seconds while I composed myself.

"I'm the one who wants to apologize to you. I was so full of myself all day yesterday—after finding my dino eggs—that I was really rude, and then I was kind of silly, hanging on to Kyle at the rodeo," Katie said.

"Thanks," I said, smiling at her. "You weren't rude. You were really happy, and you should have been."

"I bet you were thinking about your dad when I started talking about mine," Katie said. "I sort of know that look you get when you do."

"I was."

"I know how that hurts."

I didn't allow many people into that private space where I held all my thoughts about my father. But Katie Cion and Booker Dibble—my two best friends—were welcome to enter whenever they chose. My mom had the key, too.

"You didn't do it, Katie. Sometimes, I just miss him more than you can imagine."

I was named Devlin after my father. He was Lulu's only son—Devlin Atwell. But when he was killed in an explosion in Paris during my mother's pregnancy, not long after they were married, my mother decided to give me her surname, since she knew we would now be a family of two. That's why I'm Devlin Quick.

"Do you think about your dad a lot?" Katie asked.

"Every day," I said. "Wouldn't you?"

All I had were snapshots of him with my mother—looking so happy to be with her—or pictures from when he was growing up. I look a lot like him—tall and dark-haired. The same light eyes and smile, once I got my braces off. And I had all the incredible stories my mom liked to tell me about how smart her Devlin was, and how brave.

"It's not the same thing, Dev, but you know how my dad feels about you. You're like a second daughter to him. He'd do anything for—"

"Thanks, Katie." I was grateful to her dad, but no one could ever replace my own father, in my mind.

"You're going to do it, Dev. I feel sure," Katie said. "You're going to find his killers."

My dad had been a journalist—an investigative reporter for the *Wall Street Journal*. He'd covered international politics and been in war zones around the world. A lot of people thought—and Lulu was one of them—that he'd been working undercover as a spy for the CIA, but my mother told me to ignore that idea.

I'd sworn to Katie and to Booker that I would devote myself to finding out who killed my dad. I knew that all my sleuthing was practice for the day I could take on that job for real.

My mom, Blaine, had been a major crimes prosecutor before she was appointed to be the police commissioner. She had a reputation for being fierce and fair and fearless—at least, that's what Mayor Bloomfield said about her the day she was sworn in. I don't think she would have flinched at the sight of a scorpion or a rattler. I admired everything about her, and would settle for fair and fearless if I could follow in her shoes. I'd leave the fierce quality to others.

If anyone could solve the cold case of my father's murder before I got old enough to do it, it would be my mother.

"I guess you don't want to talk about it anymore," Katie said, pausing for a few seconds. "I understand that. So what are we going to do this week?"

"I'm going to sleep really late, for sure."

"Me too."

"I'll probably hit some balls in Central Park with Booker," I said. He was on the Hunter High School tennis team—the best public school in the city. "Then go to my grandmother's for dinner."

"Do you have swim practice this week?"

"Yes. I can't wait to get back in the pool."

It was always quiet when I did my laps in the Ditchley pool. Once I dove in the water, all the chatter and bad thoughts that swirled around me seemed to evaporate. I focused on my stroke and my speed and got totally in the zone where I was most comfortable.

"Once you tell me your practice schedule, we can pick the days to hang out together," Katie said.

She reached out her hand and linked her pinkie with mine. I smiled. It was a familiar move and a sign of our friendship. I squeezed her finger tightly.

"Deal," I said. "I know my first workout is Monday. Not sure about the rest."

"I'll check the movies that are playing," she said. "You go back to your book."

"Long John Silver. He's a really good villain," I said. "A pirate with one leg and a very old parrot."

"Is the parrot crested?" Katie said, playfully jabbing me in my side. "Could be related to my dinos, you know."

I laughed. "Maybe so."

I saved the last few chapters of the book to read for when I got into bed later on. When I liked a book, I wanted to stretch out the ending for as long as I could—to stay in the story and mingle with the characters. Every good book opened another world to me.

We landed at LaGuardia Airport at 6:30 p.m. Katie and I grabbed our carry-on luggage and followed Mrs. Cion off the plane, through the terminal, and downstairs to baggage claim.

We were walking toward the carousel to wait for our luggage when I spotted my mother coming toward us.

Sam Cody, her detective bodyguard and great friend, was a couple of steps behind her.

I broke into a run, dropping my bag when I reached her. I threw my arms around her neck and hung on to her for as long as I could, until she broke away and held me at arm's length.

"You don't look half bad for an Annie Oakley wannabe, Dev," she said. "Can you ride a horse yet?"

"I missed you so much, Mom," I said, kissing her on the cheek before wrapping my arms around Sam Cody. "You too, Sam."

She greeted Katie's mom and gave Katie a big hug, too.

"You won't believe what Katie found yesterday, Mom. I think she's going to have her own wing at the museum."

I was babbling on to her and to Sam about the small bones and Ling's teeth and the clutch of eggs. The trail hikes and horseback rides, learning to fish and river rafting—all of which had been so much fun—took a definite backseat to our two-day dino dig.

"I told Dev we'd save you a trip to the airport, Blaine," Mrs. Cion said. "I told her I'd ordered a car service to take us all home."

"I know that," my mother said, flashing her warmest grin. "Sam and I just finished up at a crime scene a bit ago, and I was anxious to see Dev for myself. You know how that is."

Except when my mom was away on business, or I went off with Lulu for a grandmotherly spree, we didn't spend much time apart.

"I understand completely. Dev's back in one piece, Blaine. We never saw the first bear, despite the girls' fear."

"I know I overreacted," my mother said, "but once the sheriff called me, I—"

"The *sheriff* called you?" Katie and I shouted out the words at exactly the same time.

"The Sweet Grass County sheriff?" I asked. "Why would he do that? Just because I fell in some mud?"

Mrs. Cion didn't look pleased. "You girls told me it was no big deal."

"I wanted to tell you, Mom, when we were at the rodeo. I started to say that Kyle saved Dev's life."

"She did try, Mrs. Cion," I said. "I'm the one who stopped her from telling. I figured if Katie told you, you'd tell my mom, and I had sort of hoped that wouldn't be necessary."

"Your life?" my mother asked, gripping my arm. "Someone had to save your life?"

Our quiet little reunion was becoming a frantic melee.

"Calm down, everybody," Sam said.

"It was a mudflat, Mom. Kyle pulled me out of it and I'm fine."

I didn't need to tell her that at the time I was sinking down, I wasn't sure I'd see the sunset that night. She had a pretty good imagination of her own.

"Devlin, you'd better spill the beans," Sam said. "Everything that went on."

Sam and Lulu were the only people who almost always used my proper name. I liked that.

"Why did the sheriff call?" I asked. "Professional courtesy?"

"He called to tell me that you girls were witnesses to a trespass on the dig site," my mother said.

"We weren't witnesses to anything, Mom!" I said, standing my ground, a bit louder than I should have been. "We saw tracks in the dirt the next day. No people, no evidence of a crime."

"How shaky were your observations?" Sam asked, winking at me. "Was it after the earth almost swallowed you up, Detective Quick?"

"Just before that, to be exact, Sam. All Katie and

I have is circumstantial evidence, and we weren't the least bit shaky at that point," I said. "No one knows if anything was taken."

"You girls didn't tell me about that, either," Esther Cion said. "A crime at the dig site? I'd never have approved of this trip. I don't know what my husband was thinking."

"You're not grounding me, Mom, are you?" I asked. "I promise we didn't do anything wrong. Katie was really the star of the whole operation."

"Of course you're not grounded," my mother said. "But you will have to cooperate with the sheriff, girls."

"You mean we have to go back to Big Timber?" Katie lit up, no doubt thinking of Kyle Lowry.

"No. But you'll have to come to One PP with me on Monday. Sam will monitor a call between each of you and the sheriff."

The address of the NYPD headquarters was One Police Plaza, although most detectives liked to joke that the letters stood for the Puzzle Palace.

"But Dev's got swim practice," Katie said, her voice coming close to a whine.

"There's nothing more important than solving a crime, Katie," I said. "I'll catch up on my crawl another day."

There was no place in the world—well, maybe a library

or a pool or the Museum of Natural History—that I loved to be more than in the Puzzle Palace. It was my mother's workplace, but for me it was a dazzling open house filled with smart cops and fascinating forensic tools used to investigate every kind of high crime and misdemeanor.

I was trying to hide my excitement at the prospect of roaming the halls of headquarters again—maybe getting one of the commissioner's cops to do background checks on the senior dig team members—so I looked down at the tips of my shoes and suppressed a big smile.

My mother lifted my chin to look me in the eye. I did my best to be serious. "Can I count on you, Dev? Will you come down and talk to the sheriff?"

"Sure, Mom. Katie and I will be there."

"But, Dev—" Katie interrupted again.

"I'll take care of you, Katie. We can handle this," I said. "Why don't we go check the carousel for our bags?"

It was clear my younger sidekick didn't recognize the importance of the opportunity that had fallen into our laps. I'd take her aside and convince her.

"I knew you'd be up to the task, kid," Sam said, tousling my hair. "There's a bit of the devil in you, as Sergeant Tapply likes to say. And I can always use a partner in crime."

11

I was sorely tempted to bring my shiny new miniature police badge—the one that Liza and Booker and I had each been given in a ceremony at One PP after we solved the theft at the library. But my mother said I had to keep it on my dresser at home, since it wasn't exactly the real deal.

By the time I woke up on Monday morning, it was after eight o'clock. Sam had picked my mother up at seven. Natasha was just coming back into the apartment with Asta, the dog we had rescued from a shelter two years ago, after his morning walk. It was my responsibility to walk him, but Natasha was nice enough to let me sleep in.

I stopped to scratch Asta behind his ears and tell him it was no fun to be gone without him.

"It's good to have you home, Dev," Natasha said. "You'll have to tell me all about your trip tonight."

"I'm glad to be back. Paleontology is hard work," I said, opening the refrigerator to get some juice and an English muffin.

"I bet it is."

Natasha had been orphaned as a teen in Moldova, which was once part of the Soviet Union. She'd been a victim of human trafficking—brought here to work on a farm, without pay—until the NYPD broke up the criminal ring. Then Natasha met my mother during the prosecution of the evil guys who had brought her to America. My mom admired her courage, and cared a lot that Natasha was really alone in the world. Now she lived with us—like the older sister I had longed for—while she attended Columbia University.

"Your mom said to tell you that a detective would be here to pick you, then Katie, up at ten o'clock," said Natasha. "Want me to scramble some eggs? It can give you the protein you need for your big day."

"Thanks, but I'm so egged-out from breakfast on the ranch every morning. Besides, it's not such a big deal," I said. "The discovery Katie made is so much more important than whatever the guys on the bulldozer didn't find, so far as we know."

A really nice detective from the 19th Precinct had been assigned to drive Katie and me to One PP, which was near the foot of the Brooklyn Bridge in lower Manhattan. She talked to us all the way downtown about the cases she was working on. I was pretty calm to begin with, but her stories helped keep Katie's nerves in check.

Sam had left our names at the security checkpoint outside the front door. We each showed our school IDs to the officer in charge, and he let us pass through the metal detector.

Andy Tapply met us when the elevator doors opened on fourteen.

"Hey, there. It's Quick and Cion," he said, greeting us as Katie and I stepped off. "Has the right ring for the name of a prime-time cop show, now that you're encountering trouble everywhere you go."

"Cion and Quick," Katie said, shaking Tapp's hand. "I've got the lead in this one, Sergeant. While Dev's doing laps, I'll be rehearsing for our premiere with the Ditchley drama club."

"Hey, the last thing the commissioner needs down here is drama. We've always got a little too much of that going on."

Tapp had been a sergeant in the detective division—the Major Case Unit—when my mother handpicked him to run her office. Tapp was good-natured and very smart, and always seemed to have time for me when I called.

"Your mother's downstairs in a meeting with all the borough commanders," Tapp said.

New York City is made up of five counties—separate boroughs—but with one police department that covered all of them: Manhattan, the Bronx, Brooklyn, Queens, and Staten Island.

"How about Sam?" I asked.

"He's waiting for you young ladies," Tapp said. "Did they water you out in Montana, Dev? You look an inch taller."

"They should have turned the sprinkler on me, too," Katie said, standing on her tiptoes. "I'll never catch up with her."

"Short has its virtues," I said.

"I'm not short, Dev. I'm petite."

"Well, you'll fit places I won't manage to get into. Sherlock Holmes was a much taller man than Dr. Watson."

I knew the corridors of the Puzzle Palace as well as I knew my name. No matter how many times I went to headquarters, I still got a tingle whenever I saw the gold lettering on the door to my mother's office. The words POLICE COMMISSIONER below her name were bold and bright, and they suited her well.

"The inner sanctum, girls," Tapp said, opening the door for us. "Make yourselves at home."

Sam was on his phone, standing with his back to us, looking down at the spectacular view of New York Harbor that was spread out beneath us.

"Okay if I sit at the desk?" Katie asked.

Theodore Roosevelt had once been the police commissioner of New York, back in 1895. The desk in my mother's office had belonged to him, and all my friends liked the chance to sit behind it when they visited with me.

"Absolutely," I said. "Do you want to go first?"

"You mean, talking to the sheriff?" Katie asked, running her hand over the smooth leather inlay on top of the massive wooden desk. "We can't both be on the same call at the same time?"

"Of course not, Katie. That's basic police rules," I said. "No investigator wants us mixing our ideas up. We each have to tell what we remember solo, separate from each other."

"Really, Dev? I don't remember that much."

"It will all come flooding back to you when you're in the hot seat," I said. "Trust me on that."

"Hot seat?"

"Just an expression, Katie."

That phrase had nothing to do with policing. It's what Lulu called it when she sat me down to cross-examine me about whatever I was up to.

"I'll go after you, Dev."

"Good timing, girls," Sam said, turning his attention to us. "Sheriff Brackley is in his office, and he's anxious to talk to you."

"I'll start," I said.

"Then Katie will have to hang outside there with Sergeant Tapply for a few minutes," Sam said.

"I can't even listen in?" she asked.

"I don't want to influence your memory." It sounded a little harsh, but reminded me of something my mother explained to me about how she had to deal with witnesses in real cases. "It's my turn to take a seat at Teddy Roosevelt's desk."

Sam dialed the sheriff's office from the phone on an end table next to the large sofa. When someone answered, he motioned to me to pick up the receiver on TR's desk, while he stayed on to monitor the conversation.

"Hello? This is Devlin Quick."

It turned out that I was pretty nervous after all. I hoped the gulping noise I made after I spoke my name wasn't audible.

"Devlin? Thanks for calling. This is Ryan Brackley. I'm the sheriff of Sweet Grass County," he said. "Sorry I didn't meet you when you were out here. And thanks, Sam, for getting us together."

I took the sheriff through the details of what happened on Friday morning, from the time I woke up till we went to the foot of the incline, and then when Kyle called us to point out the tire tracks.

"It's Kyle Lowry who spotted the tracks, Sheriff Brackley," I said. "And then an older girl named Ling Soo saw them next. They're the ones you ought to talk to, if you don't mind my saying."

"That's on my schedule for today, Dev."

The sheriff tried to dig deeper, but there was nothing I'd heard during the night or seen near the trail in the morning that shed any light on the episode, so I didn't feel very helpful at all. But I know a good investigator can't make any assumptions.

When he excused me, I rested the receiver on the desktop, and opened the door to change places with Katie.

"Easy as pie," I said, high-fiving her as she passed me by.

I took my cell phone out of my jeans pocket and saw

that there was a new text message. I opened it immediately. It was from Kyle.

There were two photographs attached to the text. "Here's the dozer," he had captioned the first one. "Belongs to the farmer who lives next to the dig site. It's a John Deere."

The compact-looking tractor had the green and yellow markings of that brand, and looked all shiny and new. The large bucket on the front of it was what Steve Paulson would use to excavate the Ditch for shipment to the museum.

"Here's the tire tracks this one makes."

Kyle's second photo was a close-up of the markings in the mud that the tractor had left.

"Are they a match to the photos you took on Friday?" he asked.

"Have you checked the actual site, Kyle?" I texted back.

"Can't do," he replied. A second gray bubble was forming on my iPhone screen as he wrote a longer answer. "There was a thunderstorm Saturday night and those trespasser tracks all washed out. Lucky you took a photo."

I quickly got out of the message app and opened my photos, scrolling past all the Big Sky scenery and rodeo pictures I'd taken after we left the dig.

Lucky, I thought to myself. This had nothing to do with luck. I had worked the trespass scene like a trained detective.

When I reached the Friday morning photos I'd snapped, I studied the patterns that had been left on the surface of the dirt. Then I flashed back to the incoming text from Kyle. Then back to Friday morning's markings again. Then to the new text.

"Not a match," I sent back to Kyle. "But thanks for this."

We still didn't know whether the intruder could be a different nosy neighbor looking for a valuable femur of his own, or whether this guy had more than one tractor. He sure hadn't left tracks with this colorful John Deere.

The door opened and Katie came out to where I was sitting.

"All good?" I asked.

"What a relief," she said. "The sheriff seemed like a really nice guy. And Sam was great. He told me to think carefully before I answered, and not to volunteer any information I wasn't asked."

"Sam's the best," I said.

"Yeah."

I bit my lip and hesitated before asking my question. "Katie, did you tell Sheriff Brackley about the photos I took? The ones of the tire tracks?"

"Oh, no," she said, clasping her hand over her mouth. "I forgot completely. I'll go back in and have Sam call him again."

I tugged on her belt and held her in place. "No, you won't. No need to do that."

"Why shouldn't I tell him?" Katie asked.

"'Cause we've got some detecting of our own to do first, Katie. And we're in the perfect place to do it."

12

"Okay, you two," Sam said, coming out of my mother's office and brushing past me. "Did you break the case yet?"

"Unlikely," I said.

"I'm going down to the commissioner's meeting," he said, straightening out his khaki slacks and buttoning his blazer. That was as much of a uniform as Sam needed to wear. "Are you taking off?"

"I think we'll stick around, in case my mother wants to take us to lunch," I said.

"I know that smile, Devlin Quick," Sam said. "It's not about lunch. It's about trying to impress Katie."

"Guilty!" I said, holding out my wrists to Sam. "Are you going to cuff me?"

"Don't make all the cops downstairs crazy with your investigative ideas. We have surveillance cameras all over the place in this city, but I doubt there were any that recorded the action out on the hillside in Big Timber," Sam said. "Since there was no sign of anything stolen from the site that morning, I think Sheriff Brackley is going to close the case."

"Is that what he just told you?" I said.

"Yeah."

"That's disappointing, but it makes sense," I said. "Hey, Sam? Will you ask the guys in the Real Time Crime Unit if I can let them explain to Katie how it works there? I mean, just till you and Mom come back up for lunch."

"Will do," he said. "Why? Have you got a super-duck with a rap sheet? A prehistoric arrest record?"

Katie and I had told Sam all about the dig on our way home from the airport the other night.

"There were bunches of Jurassic felons in those movies you used to take us to, Sam," Katie said. "Real man-eating dinos in those theme parks. Once we get a positive ID on my fossils, we might have to check them out."

"Fair enough. Just don't make any arrests until I come back."

"You've got it," I said.

I wrote my mother a note telling her that I was going to be showing Katie around and gave it to Tapp.

"You need a guide?" he asked.

"The Real Time Crime Center's on the eighth floor, isn't it?" I said.

"Still there."

"I can find it," I said. "I'd like to show it to Katie."

"Good idea. Like your mom says," Tapp added, "it's the beating heart of headquarters. And your buddy Richie is in charge."

"Yes! He was a great help to Liza and me," I said to Katie.

"Don't work him too hard, Dev," Tapp said. "I'll call you when the commissioner is back."

"May we each have a steno pad?" I asked.

"You two taking notes?"

"Sometimes a factoid comes up that I can use in class, Tapp. And the equipment makes us look much more professional—like real cops—than just doing it on our phones. Don't you think?"

"I guess so," he said, reaching into his drawer for two pads and pencils.

"Thanks," I said, turning to take Katie down the hallway and back to the elevators.

"So what are we up to, Dev?" Katie asked as the elevator went down to eight.

"We are going, my friend, to the technology nerve center of the NYPD."

"One of your mom's brilliant ideas, right?"

"Well, the guy before her started it, but she's made

it so much better. And there's nothing else like it anywhere in the whole country."

The doors opened and I led us around the corner, past the Technical Assistance Response Unit—we didn't need any wiretap info yet—and into Real Time Crime.

"You must be Devlin Quick," a woman in a blue uniform said when Katie and I entered. "Sam Cody just called us. I'm sorry but Richie Marcus isn't going to be in all week."

"That's too bad, "I said, pursing my lips. "I was hoping someone could give us a tour."

"I'm studying for the lieutenant's test," she said, pointing to the thick book on the table in front of her. "Let me get someone else to do that."

She walked away, into the huge room in which dozens of elite officers sat in front of enormous screens, 24/7, analyzing maps and satellite images of the city, helping cops on the street prevent and solve crimes in real time.

"It's bad that Mr. Marcus isn't here?" Katie asked.

I smiled. "It's so much better for us, actually. Richie was the guy who helped Liza and me last month. Only he didn't know he was helping us when he gave us the information we needed, so I'm not sure he'd be all that happy to see me again," I said. "I think he's a bit afraid of my mother."

The uniformed woman returned with another officer and introduced us. "This is P.O. Nieves. Sonia Nieves."

Katie and I told her our names. "We're just waiting for my mother to take us to lunch. She made us come in today because we're trying to help a sheriff out in Montana with a trespass case that happened when we were there last week," I said, trying to get Sonia interested in our cause.

Sonia Nieves was just the ticket—bright and eager and friendly. The other officer went back to her studies, but Sonia was ready to jump in with us.

"So you two are sheriff's deputies?" Sonia said, with a pat on my back. "Do you know what we've got here?"

"A ton of stuff they don't have in Big Timber, Montana," I said. "That's for sure."

"I know Dev has been here lots of times, but can you please tell me what you do in Real Time Crime?" Katie asked.

"First I'll do that," Sonia said. "Then I'll put you to work so you can see for yourself."

"That would be amazing," Katie said.

"I admire your mom so much, Dev," Sonia said. "I've only been on the job for two years, but the idea that I can even dream, as a young woman, about becoming the police commissioner of New York? Well, it's your mom who's responsible for letting me dream big these days."

"Me too," I said. "Would you please explain to Katie what goes on in the center?"

"You got it," Sonia said, walking us into the room, with its jaw-dropping display of equipment and giant screens. "So this is where it all happens. We've got fifteen workstations, which are staffed by three dozen analysts and investigators who work around the clock."

Katie let out a low whistle, taking it all in.

"It's like a mega–help desk for detectives who are on duty, in their cars or at crime scenes or in their precinct houses," Sonia said. "We provide instant information to the thirty-seven thousand police officers who keep this city safe."

"Wow," Katie said. "Big Timber only has seventeen hundred people living there, total. We've got thirty-seven thousand officers? This is just amazing."

"What the department did, girls, was upload warehouses full of data to a high-tech new system. I mean, a lot of it is information the NYPD has had for a long time, but it's been stored on shelves collecting dust."

"Now, the minute a cop contacts the center and asks for someone's criminal history," I said, "he gets an answer quicker than he could make a phone call."

"That's so much safer for the cops, and the citizens," Sonia said. "Dev's right. We've got twenty million New York City criminal complaints and 911 calls, and thirty-three billion—"

"Million?" Katie asked.

"Think big, Katie," Sonia said. "B as in boy. Billions of public records."

"Just from New York City?"

"No, Katie. They're from all over the country. And the range of the data we've collected makes it really special."

Way to go, Sonia, I thought to myself.

"Come on, girls," Sonia said. "One of you should sit down at my desk."

"You go, Dev," Katie said. "I'm not sure what we're looking for."

"What's the part of the Ditchley motto you don't understand, Katie? *We learn, we lead*," I said. "You can't always tell me to go first. You ought to lead more, especially when it involves Big Timber."

"You're more tech savvy than I am," Katie said.

"So what was the trespass?" Sonia asked. "Someone break into a house?"

"Nope."

"What then?"

"They just came on to private property, in the middle of the night, where they didn't belong."

"Land? They just trespassed on dirt, not into a house or business?" Sonia asked. "That's a tough one. Why are you two involved?"

"Katie's family has a ranch in Montana," I said. "We were there digging for dinosaur fossils."

"That sounds really neat."

"My mom's idea. She asked us to come here today in order to try to help the sheriff out there."

"We just got off the phone with him," Katie said.

"My mom thinks we can—you know—"

"I'd do anything for the commissioner," Sonia said, sitting down in front of her computer while Katie and I stood behind her.

Actually, I had counted on that reaction when we headed down here. Who in the NYPD wouldn't want to perform for Blaine Quick? Only the guys who'd spent enough time around me to know that every boundary laid out in front of me looked too tempting to ignore.

"Are you and Katie involved because you saw a possible suspect?"

“There are no suspects,” I said.

Sonia turned her head to look up at me, with a puzzled expression on her face. “So what am I supposed to do, Dev?”

“Is there anything in your databank about treads on tire tracks?”

“Bingo!” Sonia said. “Now I can show off some bells and whistles.”

Sonia’s fingers moved as fast as red ants chasing chocolate bits over the keyboard. When she hit Enter, a program title popped up on her screen in all caps—WHEELS OF PROGRESS.

Then she yelled out so the other detectives working beneath the huge screens could hear her. “I’m taking screen six,” Sonia said. “Breaking news in Montana.”

The city street scene disappeared from the overhead screen twenty feet in front of us and an image of six tires, each one of them blown up, way larger than life-size, appeared in its place.

Katie blinked and looked again. “Why would you have a database entry full of giant tires, Sonia?”

“Crime scene investigation work,” Sonia said. “Think of all the car accidents in a big city. When there’s a hit and run, often the only evidence we have is the image of the tire track left on the pavement—sometimes because it's preserved on an oily surface, or a bloody one."

"Can I show you what we've got?" I asked.

"Don't hold back, Dev."

I pulled up the text of the tire that Kyle had sent not long ago, and Sonia told me how to forward it to her computer and bring it up on the larger screen as well. Then she stood up.

"Do it yourself, young lady," Sonia said. "The image of your tire is up there. Do you know what kind of vehicle it's on?"

"Yes, ma'am," I said. "It's on a John Deere compact tractor. I can see from the photograph I got today that the model number is F-1802."

"How do you know that?" Katie said, clamping her hand on my shoulder. "We never saw any machine on Friday."

"Kyle just texted me while you were talking with Sheriff Brackley," I said. "This is the vehicle that Steve brought in—"

"Wait a minute," Katie said, obviously stuck on my mention of Kyle's name. "He texted *you*? What about me?"

"It's not personal, Katie. It's investigative stuff," I said, not wanting to get in that sweet space between a pal and her first serious crush. "This is the truck that

Steve arranged for after we left to pick up the Ditch filled with your clutch of eggs."

"Do your thing, Dev," Sonia said. "Go to John Deere on that website—that's your vehicle type—and key in the model number."

I did that, looking at the list of options the menu offered me. I didn't want to buy one, that's for sure. I just wanted to see which tires fit it.

I skipped sales and repairs and replacement parts, and clicked on the word "Tires." Three images appeared on the small computer screen, with noticeably different patterns on their treads.

I leaned in to study the treads on the image Kyle sent—six lines of indentations in the rubber circling around the tire, with diamond-shaped detail on each side of the lines.

"That's a match, Sonia," I said. "It's just like the one on the far left."

"Double click on it," she said.

When I did, the tire I selected showed up instantly on the big screen, alongside the tracks from the dino dig's John Deere.

"What have you got?" Sonia asked.

"This is like magic," I said, reading the small print. "The tire is made by a company called Carlisle. It's their

All-Trail II model. It fits most compact-size riding tractors."

"Once again, it's Kyle to the rescue," Katie said.

I was glad I was facing the computer screen. I didn't want Katie to see me gagging while she heaped all the praise on her cowboy.

"Does that solve your problem?" Sonia asked.

"Not at all," I said glumly, placing my chin in my hands. "But now I'm stuck with the reverse situation."

"You mean a tire you want to identify?" Sonia asked.

"Yep."

"Figure it out, Dev. Throw your photo up on the screen," Sonia said.

I transferred the snapshot I took last Friday to Sonia's computer, and then pitched it up to the giant screen.

This tire that left this impression in the earth also had distinctive treads. There were double rows of indentations in the print made by the rubber, and double lines that intersected the long ones, spread an inch apart, all around the tire circumference. There were some open patches in the dirt where the tires had been, either from bald spots on the rubber or because the imprint hadn't been firmly made.

I thought for a couple of seconds. "Don't tell me, okay?" I asked Sonia.

In the search area of the site, I typed in the word "tread." Within fifteen seconds, the database spit out almost a thousand images.

I narrowed the search this time, describing the double lines in both directions.

Suddenly there were only four tires left that fit the description. I enlarged each image to sit side by side with my own photograph on the big screen.

I featured them one at a time. When the third one was blown up beside my picture, Katie was the first of us to shriek that the patterns matched.

"That's it, Dev! Now figure out the rest," she said. "If that machine sitting on top of those tires is anywhere in Sweet Grass County, I bet you Kyle can find it."

"Kyle's the sheriff?" Sonia asked.

"Something like that," I said. "We can give him a call when we're done."

I trusted Kyle, just like Katie did, and he might be our best bet to do some necessary undercover work without bothering Sheriff Brackley, who'd already told Sam he was inclined to close the case.

I would try to do this without asking Sonia. I right-clicked on the image of the tire and the computer in front of me brought up a new folder.

"The Atlas Road Warrior," I said. "Very distinctive."

I clicked again on one of the headings that said MATCHING VEHICLES.

The photograph displayed showed two riding machines—a mower and a compact bulldozer, much like the John Deere—but this one was dark gray with red lettering.

I ignored the mower and enlarged the dozer, then read aloud to Katie and Sonia.

"'Atlas Road Warrior tires are compatible with all Atlas compact vehicles. We do not recommend any other brand for use with our machines.'"

"That will certainly narrow the search," Sonia said, looking over my shoulder. "Atlas is a much smaller company than John Deere, so there are likely to be fewer of them out there. Good work, Dev."

"What's next?" Katie asked.

"I can call that sheriff for you," Sonia said. "You know, one professional to another."

I should have given Sonia cred for her years on the job, but we kids had formed a special bond.

"Thanks so much. I promised my mother I'd handle this for Katie and me. Mom's working on my maturity, if you know what I mean. Accepting responsibility for things I do. She's pretty tough about that."

"Of course," Sonia said, palms out in my direction as she backed away from us.

I dialed Kyle's cell. When he didn't pick up, I figured that he was out of range on the dig hillside, but would hear my message when he got back in town.

"Hey, Kyle. It's Katie and me. Well, it's me. Dev. You're looking for a dark gray tractor that says ATLAS ROAD WARRIOR in bright red on its side," I said. "If you find it, Kyle, keep the word under that big hat of yours until we talk. Bye for now."

13

"Time to spare," I said, checking the time on my phone, after thanking Sonia and retracing our steps. "No word from Sam yet, and Tapp's for sure gone to lunch."

"Now what?"

"Your turn to empower yourself, Katie," I said. "Seat yourself in Sergeant Tapply's well-worn chair."

"What if he comes back?"

"What you're about to do is perfectly legal," I said.

"Sure?"

"I'd never mislead you, Katie. You're my best buddy."

Katie's small frame seemed swallowed up when she sank into the soft cushion on Tapp's chair.

"Type in CLEAR—in all caps. That's the program you're going to work in."

"Don't I need a password?" she asked.

"Tapp's password is Lady Blue, for my mom. First woman commish in the long blue line of the NYPD."

"Neat name," Katie said. "Now what?"

"Search for Steve Paulson."

"You don't think he has a criminal record, do you?" Katie said, wrenching her neck to look back at me.

"CLEAR is a national log of personal information about people, from all kinds of sources—motor vehicles, employment, education. It's not about arrest records."

"So I won't go to jail for looking at this, right?" Katie asked.

"Perfectly legal. It's just too expensive for people to pay for this program on their home computers, or trust me, I'd download it tonight," I said. "The only person who'd lock us up for doing this is my mom. So make it snappy."

"I'm typing as fast as I can."

"I just want to know more about everyone at that dig. I doubt Steve's a perp-paleontologist."

Katie typed in Paulson's name. Several others spelled just like it popped up, but there was only one who lived in Bozeman and was an associate curator at the Museum of the Rockies.

"Scroll down," I said.

"Forty-six years old," Katie read out loud. "Married with three kids. He's published two books about dinosaurs—and wow, about twenty-seven articles in magazines."

"He drives a '14 Ford Bronco," I said. "Too bad you

don't need a license to operate a tractor or we'd have a head start looking for our Road Warrior."

"It's got his address and all his degrees," Katie said. "But look at this, Dev. Steve Paulson was fired—from some museum with a Spanish name. I don't understand it."

"Really?" I said, looking over Katie's shoulder to write down the foreign words in my NYPD steno pad.

"Doesn't 'terminated' mean 'fired'?" she asked.

"I guess so. I mean it could just mean the project he was working on ended, and that he completed it," I said.

"Or else he was fired," Katie said. "I wonder what he did?"

"Read that. It looks like whatever Steve did, he did it in Patagonia," I said, "which is Argentina."

"Actually, Patagonia is part of Chile," Katie said. "My brother went there on a ski trip last year. It's at the very southern tip of South America."

"I'm pretty sure it's part of both countries, but I'll ask Liza," I said. "She'll know exactly where Patagonia is."

I should have realized that mentioning Liza's name would put Katie into a full-on snit.

"You don't need Liza de Lucena for that, Dev. You just need Google."

"Never mind. I'll look it up when I get home tonight,

Katie," I said. "How about Chip Donner? See what you can find out about him."

Donner was a pretty common surname. A list of hundreds of them rolled out on the screen, but none had the first name of Chip.

"Could be his nickname," Katie said. "I keyed in Montana and dozens of Donners still spring up. Do I have to go through them all?"

"That will take too long for now," I said. "We'll come back to him if we have time. Maybe you can ask Kyle more about him. Why don't we see whether Ling Soo shows up?"

"Here we go again," Katie said. "That's a really common Chinese surname. Do you know how old she is?"

"We don't have her date of birth, but try someone who's about twenty-two or twenty-three."

"Where from?" Katie asked.

"I never asked her," I said. "Type in Gobi Desert. We know she's been there on a dig. I bet there aren't many people who can claim that."

"It worked, Dev! Look at this."

The description sure sounded like our Ling Soo. She was twenty-five years old, born in a small city in China, educated in archaeology and paleontology at a university in Beijing, and author of a *National Geographic* article on juvenile duckbills.

"I've got to get busy and write up a piece on my clutch," Katie said, clapping her hands together. "What if I could be published before I'm even twelve?"

"You're going to be twelve on Saturday. You'd better hunker down and tell your story if you think that's in the cards. When we see Ling—when she gets to New York—you can ask her for help."

Katie buried her nose in the computer screen again. "Hey, Dev? Didn't Ling tell us she was a grad student at Yale?"

"Yes, she did. Several times," I said. "Why?"

"This page says she entered the graduate program in Yale almost two years ago," Katie said. "But she withdrew in the middle of the last semester."

"Withdrew?"

"Yeah, not terminated. Nothing like that."

"Does it give any reason for the withdrawal?" I asked.

"Nope. That's the last word on her page," Katie said. "We'll just have to ask her that when we see her."

I didn't want to blow the surprise about Katie's party, but I was too excited to stay quiet. "That could be much sooner than you think!"

14

Katie and I were sitting on either side of Teddy Roosevelt's desk—talking about his transition from police commissioner to Rough Rider during the Spanish-American War—when my mother and Sam returned from their meeting.

"Have you two been amusing yourselves?" she asked. "Keeping out of trouble?"

I got out of her chair, held it back for her to sit in, then threw my arms around her shoulders from behind her. "I've already got my gold shield, Mom. I'm moving on."

"I think Devlin's between cases, Commissioner," Sam said. "The sheriff hit a dead end with his trespass investigation, so my sidekick will have to wait for her next assignment."

Lulu had taught me that it was rude to correct intelligent adults, so I just let Sam's verdict lie.

"Are we going out for lunch?" I asked.

"Oh, I'm so sorry, darling," my mother said. "Didn't you see Tapp? He's going to bring back sandwiches for you when his lunch is over."

"He'd already gone out when we got back up here after our—um—after our tour."

"One of the Staten Island ferries slammed into the dock. We've got to do a press conference on public safety with the mayor."

"Anybody hurt?" Katie asked.

"Fortunately not. But Sam and I have to run out, so you two can just relax and take charge of my office," my mother said.

She had the most engaging smile in the world. Most days I hoped that Sam noticed it, too. I knew that she needed a bodyguard, but I also wanted her to have someone to love, besides me.

"Ms. Quick," Katie said, "my mom asked me to ask you something."

"Go ahead, dear."

"Well, all I'm allowed to know about Saturday night is that we're celebrating my birthday. It's a surprise, so she won't tell me what or where," Katie said. "I know you and Dev know all about it."

"My lips are sealed," my mother said.

"Well, we were wondering if it's okay if I invite Natasha, too? I mean, my mom thinks we'd have more fun if our chaperone is—well—isn't a mom."

"She's absolutely right about that."

"So if I see Natasha this afternoon, I can ask her?"

"Of course you can."

"I love that idea," I said.

Not only would Natasha help me bake cupcakes, but she could be a great ally in the fun I was planning for the sleepover at the museum. Katie, Natasha, Booker, and a few of the Ditchley girls in the mix—my perfect posse of partygoers was growing nicely.

Shortly after my mother and Sam took off, Tapp came back with a supply of sandwiches and chips and soda.

"I hope you don't mind that I used your computer, Tapp," I said.

"You did? Thanks for telling me."

"The confession of evil deeds is the beginning of good deeds," I said, bowing at the waist to him, thanking him for our lunch.

"Where'd you get that line?" Katie asked. "Sounds kind of like your grandmother."

"I was quoting Saint Augustine, not Lulu," I said with a laugh. "If it's not Lulu's wisdom I'm relying on—or Miss Manners's—it's bound to be a saint."

"Did you find what you were looking for?" Tapp asked.

"Mostly. We were trying to get some background on the nice people who ran our dig, so that Katie can write an essay about it."

"Dev! Do *not* blame this on me," Katie said.

"What's to blame?" Tapp asked. "I'd like to read it when you're done."

"So we did fine on two of the first three people, but I may be able to get more information on another of the guys. Right now we just have his nickname," I said. "And there are some grad students Katie should acknowledge, too."

"And Kyle," she said, going along with the program.

"I think you probably know everything about him that you need to," I said to Katie, before turning back to Tapp. "Anyway, we might send you another name or two during the week."

Tapp waved us off. "Go on, eat your lunch. I got you turkey sandwiches with all the trimmings, okay? Get me any names and pedigree information you have on them, and I'll forward the results to you. Now I've got to get back to work."

We ate our lunches, took a bunch of selfies at the commissioner's desk, and then rode the subway back uptown to my apartment.

It was my turn to walk Asta. By the time we squared the block and got back upstairs, Natasha had come home from school.

"Are you busy Saturday night?" Katie asked her, after we told her some of the stories about our trip to Montana.

"No plans that are carved in stone. Why?"

"My mom has organized some kind of birthday surprise, and we're going to need to have a grown-up with us," Katie said. "I'd love for you to be the adult. It'd be much more fun than having a parent there."

"I'm so flattered," Natasha said, exchanging high fives with Katie. "Of course I'll do it."

Natasha went into her room, while Katie and I just hung out for a few more hours, Instagramming our photos from headquarters.

"Can you believe there are only five more days till I'm twelve?" she asked, when she got ready to leave for home. "I'm really excited about it."

"Me too," I said. "I've got swim practice tomorrow and Thursday. Maybe we can do something together on Friday?"

"Sure."

"Don't forget to call Kyle," I said. "He has to help us with two things."

"Two?"

"He needs to find us someone near the dig site, or in town, who has an Atlas Road Warrior," I said. "And he's got to find out Chip Donner's real name and pedigree information."

"Pedigree?" Katie asked. "Like a dog?"

I would have to stop rolling my eyes when I lost it with my friends. I knew it was a bad habit.

"In law enforcement, we use the word 'pedigree' to refer to the vital statistics of our witnesses and suspects. The more specifics you can ask Kyle to get about Chip and Steve and Ling and the rest of the crew, the more info we can gather. Dates of birth, addresses, cars they own—those things make up a pedigree. Get specifics, okay?"

"Got it."

"I'll talk to you later," I said, sort of distracted from what we had been talking about and feeling in a bit of a funk. We were walking to the door and saying goodbye.

"You seem kind of down, Dev. Is it—?"

"Nothing serious this time, Katie. I didn't mean to go dark on you," I said. "I'm just bummed since Sheriff Brackley closed the case today. I need something to do to keep me busy."

"You know my mom, Dev. It's only a matter of days until she loses an earring or leaves her iPad in a taxi. You'll be up and running again soon."

"Well, I won't hold my breath waiting for bad things to happen to other people" I said.

I spread out on the living room floor, grabbing a pillow from the sofa and putting my hair up in an elastic to get it out of the way. I ignored the raindrops that were beginning to pound against the window. My mother had given me a three-volume biography of Eleanor Roosevelt, insisting that I read the life story of the first presidential wife to have a career of her own. It was actually interesting from the earliest days of Eleanor's childhood. I loved dense books that could hold my attention for days on end.

I was so deep into the story that I didn't realize my mother had come into the apartment until she bent down and tugged on my ponytail.

"You've started the book?" she said, blowing me a kiss.

"I didn't know she was TR's niece," I said. "And that her name was Eleanor Roosevelt—I mean, before she married Franklin—that's the name she was born with. Eleanor Roosevelt Roosevelt. That's weird, Mom."

"Franklin was her cousin. A distant cousin."

"Even weirder, don't you think?"

"It worked out just fine in the end, Dev."

"You wouldn't like it if I was Devlin Quick Quick, would you?"

"For entirely different reasons, dear," my mother said. "You don't really know all your distant relatives like I do."

"Can we talk about that?"

"Someday."

"That's so parental," I said. "'Someday' and 'maybe' are the two most common parental put-offs in the language."

"How do you feel about pizza for dinner?"

"Excellent. Most excellent," I said. "But you and Natasha like too many things on your pizza. Please get me some plain slices, will you?"

My mother and Lulu thought my picky eating was just a phase I would outgrow. But I didn't like having things on my pizza like red peppers or veggies that cluttered up the cheese, and I really don't like those wormlike creatures—anchovies—crawling around in my salad.

I kind of enjoyed this lazy week, more than I'd thought I would. I'd gone straight from the end of the semester to Ditchley's summer school—with homework just like it was the real deal—and then right out to Montana without any kind of a break.

It was sweet to have dinners with my mom and Natasha, just sitting around the kitchen table, and Wednesday had been an especially fun night when we went out for thick juicy steaks with Sam. It wasn't often that Mom could clear the decks of police emergencies and put together a string of family evenings.

On Thursday, Natasha roasted a chicken and made mashed potatoes—my favorite meal—and we waited till eight o'clock to eat, because my mother got called to a crime scene on the Lower East Side. She told us about the case—a home invasion—while I washed the dishes, and then we went into the living room to watch the ten o'clock local news.

"Are you going to be on TV?" I asked my mother.

"Not if I can help it, Dev," she said, settling in on the sofa.

I stretched out on the other end and put my feet in her lap. "I love it when you look all serious and go 'no comment' to the newsmen."

"It's the right thing to do, dear. The detectives and I don't know enough to say anything early on, and we don't want to say something we might regret by the time a crime scene is examined and the witnesses are interviewed," she explained, massaging my aching calves while she talked. "The facts should come out in a courtroom, not off the cuff."

Natasha clicked on the television and flipped to the station we liked to watch.

After the commercial, the anchor opened the newscast: "We have a lot to tell you about tonight, so we're going to start with breaking news."

"They must have made an arrest in your case," Natasha said to my mother.

"No." She sat up straighter but didn't flinch. "I would have been notified by the chief of detectives if that had happened."

One thing about my mom—she hated to be the last to know.

"You can see that our reporter is on the front steps of the American Museum of Natural History," the anchor said.

I twisted onto my side to stare at the screen. My mother, on the other hand, relaxed and kept rubbing my legs. The newsman was standing beneath the huge statue of Theodore Roosevelt on horseback. He was so close to the horse's hooves I thought he might get kicked in the head if he didn't hurry up and get to the point.

"Those Roosevelts are everywhere," I said.

"Ssssssh." Natasha was into the moment.

"I'm standing at the entrance to the American Museum of Natural History—one of New York's most iconic institutions, visited by more than five million people every year—where the museum's president just made a startling announcement."

The cameraman panned the historic facade of the museum, to increase the dramatic effect of the announcement.

"I hope he isn't going to blow the surprise about Katie's birthday party," I said.

"Not what I'd call breaking news," Natasha said, reaching back to poke my leg.

"Not *he*, darling," my mother said. "Ms. Sutton is the first woman president of your favorite museum."

"Like you!" I said.

My mother laughed. "Like me, Dev. Only smarter. Wicked smart, as the Boston Quicks would say."

The engraving over the entrance was strong but simple: TRUTH. KNOWLEDGE. VISION.

"Earlier tonight," the newsman said, "President Sutton stood on these steps with several scientists to announce the findings that support the probable existence of an entirely new species of dinosaurs, unknown to paleontologists until the discovery less than one week ago in the Badlands of Montana."

I was on my feet, digging into the cushions to find my phone to call Katie.

"Mom!" I was so excited I could barely catch my breath. "Mom! This could be the crested duckbill Steve was looking for. And Katie's clutch of eggs might be the find of the century. She's going to be so famous!"

"Listen in," the reporter said, playing a tape of the earlier interview from the museum's front steps.

President Sutton was at the microphone attached to a temporary podium, surrounded by a group of people whom I recognized immediately.

"That's Steve Paulson," I said, kneeling down in front of the screen and pointing at him. "And Chip Donner. And that's Ling Soo."

". . . . and our team of expert paleontologists," Sutton went on, "will be working with this group, who flew in with their fossils today, so that we can begin the painstaking work of confirming the identity of this ancient animal. It's quite possible that the bones you are looking at, ladies and gentlemen, are the first feathered dinosaur fossils in the world—the long-sought proof of a firm link between birds and dinosaurs."

"You didn't tell us about feathers," my mother said.

"Katie didn't find any such thing, Mom. This is all news to me."

President Sutton gestured to the young woman standing next to Steve. Ling moved closer to the podium.

"This marks an historic partnership in our relationship with the Chinese—forged in the Gobi Desert by one of our founding members a century ago—and revived on a hillside in Montana by this hard-working group of scientists," Sutton said, "and by the tenacity of a talented graduate student with a very bright future."

Ling Soo smiled at the camera and nodded her head, mouthing the words "thank you."

"The great Age of Exploration, celebrated by this museum for more than one hundred and fifty years, continues today, as you see here," President Sutton said. "We'll do the work to authenticate this unique find, and then invite you all to come back to the museum to see this 'terrible lizard,' which Ms. Soo will have the privilege of naming."

"LING SOO!"

"Stop screaming, Dev. The neighbors might call 911," my mother said.

"But it was Katie's big discovery," I said.

"Apparently, there was something even bigger that happened after you two left the dig. You and Katie will have to deal with this. I'm sure it's disappointing, but it doesn't take a single thing away from Katie's clutch."

"I'm telling you, Mom. There's something wrong with this picture," I said. "Ling was really jealous when Katie found her nest. I sort of got the feeling that she didn't want Katie to succeed at all. She didn't want Katie to get credit for anything."

"You're being too harsh on this young woman, Dev. I'm sure Katie's eggs will be an essential part of confirming and proving Ling's discovery."

"I hope so," I said. "There's something way too mysterious about this turn of events."

"What do you mean?" Natasha asked.

"I can't put my finger on it yet," I said, trying to order the jumble of ideas racing through my brain. "No comment."

I thought of Katie and her switched bones the first night at the dig, then the tire tracks of the trespassers, and then her monumental discovery—just before we left town. I had a bad feeling about things.

"Dev?" my mother said. "Devlin Quick?"

Using my full name came first. The finger wagging was sure to follow.

"Let sleeping dinos lie, okay?" Mom was shaking her forefinger at me.

My phone was ringing. I reached between the cushions to retrieve it.

"Sure thing, Commissioner," I said to my mother heading into my bedroom to answer the call. "I read you loud and clear."

15

"*Soo-saurus*?" Katie said. "It just doesn't have the same ring as the *Cionosaurus katus*."

"The name isn't the important part," I said, closing the door to my room. "I'm beginning to think you were right."

"About what?"

"First of all, remember how upset you got the first night, when you thought that Chip Donner had swapped out your little bones?"

"I told you so."

"I hope you'll lose that expression soon, Katie. It's really an under-eight kind of thing to say."

"Saint Augustine's opinion?"

"Nope," I said. "My grandmother's. But then there's the way Ling was a weeny bit too edgy when you found the clutch. She was all about wishing she had made the discovery herself."

"But, Dev, Ling even said it was the best thing anybody could find in a dig—unhatched dinosaur eggs."

"Yes," I said, climbing up on top of my comforter and

opening my iPad with my other hand. "Then she goes ahead and the very next day she's the one who finds something even better."

"It's a bummer," Katie said. "I'm so glad I didn't waste time writing a paper about it. Looks like my precious Ditch will get buried by Ling's feathered friends."

"Don't be silly, Katie. Nothing can take away your buried treasure. I'm sure they can't prove anything without the eggs."

Katie was quiet for a moment. "You're a real friend, Dev. Thanks for saying that."

"Even my mom thinks that's true"

"Do you think Ling will keep her word? Let us visit her at the museum? I do want to see the fossils she found."

"Good idea, Katie. I'll text her, now that we know she's in New York."

"We could drop in on her tomorrow."

"I can't do that," I said. "I mean, I'm busy all day."

I had promised Mrs. Cion that I would keep Katie away from the museum until Saturday night's party. Her mother didn't want her to see any of the brand-new exhibitions that had just opened before we got our private tour for the birthday party. Not that I'd even thought for a second that Katie would want to go there this week. I figured she'd be busy locket-shopping.

"Doing what?"

"Um—Booker," I said, trying to think of an excuse. "Booker wants me to go to—um—to the Statue of Liberty with him."

"He does?" Katie asked. "You've both been there a dozen times."

"I know. I'm trying to talk him out of it. I'll let you know if our plans change," I said. "Meanwhile, have you talked to Kyle?"

"About the tractor?"

"Yeah. And about Chip's real name."

"I texted him but he hasn't answered yet."

"That's your assignment, Katie. Stay on it, okay?"

We said good night and then I texted Booker. "You up? Too late to call?"

Less than a minute later, Booker Dibble phoned me. "'Sup, Dev?"

"Hey, Booker. What are you doing tomorrow?"

"Hanging out with some of my friends from Hunter. Why?"

"You'll have all the school year to do that," I said. "I'm thinking of doing some investigative work."

"I've already got a gold shield, Dev," he said to me. "What more does a guy want?"

"I think Katie needs a save."

"You told me all about finding her clutch. She should be sitting on top of the world."

"She was, Booker," I said. "But somebody just knocked her off. Humpty Dumpty and all that. You and I have to put her back together again."

I told him the update of the story I'd given him earlier in the week.

"What do you want to do about it?" he asked.

"I thought we could go over to the museum tomorrow and look for Ling. I have a lot of questions I want to ask her. I can't take Katie with me because it would spoil the whole surprise that Mrs. Cion is trying to pull off."

"Do you know for sure that Ling will be there?"

"Nope. But all the fossils from the dig—and Katie's clutch—are there. I heard the museum president say so on the news just a few minutes ago."

"Nobody's going to give two kids access to those old bones, Dev."

"Everybody trusts *you*, Booker. You've got 'reliability' written all across your face," I said. "That's why I like to have you on my side of things."

My compliment was met with silence.

"At least we could scope the place out before Saturday night, Booker. The truth is that because Katie found her fossils on private property, they actually belong to her. Mrs. Cion told my mom that Katie's dad called the ranch owner, who was happy to let her have them. That's going to be one of her birthday surprises," I said. "So if Katie asked for them back from the museum, they would have to let her have them."

"Are you pulling a waggles?" Booker asked.

"No, sir. No lie at all. Not even a fiblet."

"So you have a plan to get some of the bones back?"

"I can't say it's come together as a formulated plan," I said. "But I'll sleep on it."

"What would you do with a fossil, Dev?"

"I've been thinking about that," I said. It was always cool to test one of my theories on a sympathetic sleuth. "I was figuring I could get my mom to have it analyzed at the DNA lab."

Booker laughed. "Let me guess, Dev. You haven't asked her to do that yet, right?"

"Baby steps, Booker. No point asking before the bones are in reach."

"And what exactly will the DNA tests tell you?"

I didn't have an answer for that one, either. I was hoping the paleontologists would give me a good reason. Probable cause is what my mother would want, to get the city's DNA lab involved. It was a legal term that was worse than "someday" or "maybe."

"We might find out who had their mitts on the fossils," I said.

"That's what fingerprints are for."

"DNA is more reliable than that, Booker."

"Well—but—"

"Katie's prints might have been on the bones the first night. But then when she passed them along to other people, their own fingerprints would cover up most traces of hers."

"And DNA?" Booker asked.

"A person's DNA can be on an object like a bone because our skin cells come off—they rub off onto things we touch. And no matter how many other people touch the same thing after we do, there's a good chance that our DNA—just a tiny fragment of it—will still show up."

"Trace evidence," he said. "We learned about it in biology last year."

"So I'm thinking of getting to the museum about one o'clock tomorrow afternoon, Booker. What do you say about that?"

I couldn't see Booker's face, of course, but I knew he was smiling.

"Game on, Devlin Quick. Game on."

16

"I may not be able to sleep at all tomorrow night," I said, talking to Booker as we walked through the great hall of North American mammals on the first floor of the museum.

"Why not?"

"Just in case these animals in the dioramas come to life. It reminds me of being in a tent in Montana."

We passed glass display case after glass display case—grizzly bears, mountain lions, panthers, moose, and elk—all real animals that had once been alive, displayed against scenery that resembled their natural habitat.

"You want me to bring a bow and arrow to the party?" Booker asked.

"Only if you think the smell of Natasha's cupcakes will bring them out of their long slumber."

"You're safe. The cupcakes will be eaten by us by the time those animals break out of their cases. Besides, that only happens in the movies," he said. "Did you text Ling to say you were coming?"

"No. I kind of like the element of surprise. Sam says it's a real advantage for detectives."

"Where to, then?" Booker asked.

When we entered the museum, we had each picked up one of the floor plans. We turned into a stairwell and I spread my map out across a broad step.

"Aren't most of the dinosaurs on the fourth floor? On top?" I said.

"Yeah."

"Well, if we start there, I'm sure someone can direct us to the lab," I said. "Elevators?"

"Too slow," Booker said. "Start climbing."

Every schoolkid in New York—and just about every tourist—considered the natural history museum a required stop. Almost everything I knew about animals and birds; origins of Native American, African, and Pacific peoples; sources of gems, minerals, and meteorites, I learned within these massive walls.

"You know what my mom told me this morning?" I asked. "That this museum is actually a whole bunch of different buildings, built at all different times."

Booker was taller than I was by half a head. He was taking the steps two at a time, and I imagined I could hear Katie, yelling at us to slow down. He was African American—and had once pointed out to me, when I was maybe five or six, that our ancestors occupied different "halls" in this vast museum.

"You told Aunt Blaine that we were coming here?" Booker asked.

His mother and mine had been college roommates—best friends since the age of eighteen—so we called them "aunts" even though we weren't related.

"I did."

Booker stopped on the landing and looked down at me. "She was okay with it?"

"Somebody has to pick out a place for us to sleep at Katie's party, right? Under the humongous blue whale, or in the room with the T. rex? I told Mrs. Cion I'd help with the choices she has," I said. "My mom was fine with my doing that."

"It works for me," Booker said. "What was her point about all these buildings?"

"You know how big this place is, when you stand at the entrance on Central Park West, where Roosevelt's statue is? Well, that wasn't even the first part that was built."

"No way."

"You can see that the bricks are different," I said. "The original entrance from the eighteen seventies was on Seventy-Seventh Street. So even though these buildings connect in the great hallways where all the exhibits are, when you go into the basements, each one of them is a dead end. Twenty-eight separate structures, with every kind of dead animal in each one of them."

"I've had enough of basements," Booker said, pointing above us to the next flight. "We're going upward this time."

I knew, when he said no basements, that he was thinking about our last case.

"I just thought it was interesting," I said.

"Creepy things always interest you, Dev."

I poked my head out of the stairwell when we reached the third floor. There were endless cabinets of birds on display, and beyond them were the exhibits of primates, reptiles, and amphibians.

We reached the fourth-floor landing and snapped our fingers, smiling at our touchdown. We'd reached dino headquarters—practically an entire floor, covering several city blocks, where all the remains of the ancient fossils were gathered.

No matter how many times I visited the museum, it excited me as much as it did the first time I went. The scientists' knowledge expanded and evolved, the exhibits were updated and remounted, and the excitement of seeing something for the first time never got old.

I went up to the first security guard we saw, at the

entrance to the room with triceratops and asked him how to get to the dinosaur laboratory.

"I have no idea what you're talking about, young lady. There's nothing like that on this floor."

Booker was winding his way among all the different horned monsters, stopping to admire several along the way.

"Excuse me," I said, stopping a woman in a security uniform in the middle of the Vertebrate Origins display. "You've got a lab here where your staff works on processing old bones."

"A lab?" she asked. "Take the elevator down to the ground floor and then find an entrance to the basement beneath the Astor turret. It goes four stories deep below the ground. There're a lot of bones down there."

"I said no basements, Dev," Booker said. "Not without a police escort."

"I'm actually looking for *newer* old bones," I said to the guard. "Ones that just arrived here this week. They're in some kind of laboratory."

"Most of the labs are way underground," she said. "There may be a couple upstairs."

"The museum has a fifth floor?" Booker asked.

"Just in some places, where you see the turrets from the outside," the guard said.

"How do we get up to them?" Booker said.

The older woman cocked her head and stared at my friend head-on. "You got some kind of special pass, young man?"

"I'm just a student," he said. "What kind of pass do I need?"

"The labs aren't open to the public," she said. "That's why they're not on that floor plan of yours. You've got to show fifth-floor security something that says you work here."

I elbowed Booker aside and tried to make our connection more personal. "I've got a friend who's doing her internship here. Can't we just go up and say hello to her?"

The guard thought about it. "I wouldn't even know where to direct you."

I needed more help from Booker. If he'd only use what my grandmother called his Dibble-Dazzle smile, I knew the lab doors would swing open.

I prodded him again and he got the point.

"We promise not to stay long," he said, flashing a grin. "Just doing a 'hi-and-bye' kind of thing, ma'am. We're looking for a friend whose name is Ling Soo."

That smile and a bit of name-dropping to show we really had a friend here got us further than any special pass ever could.

"I'll tell you what," she said. "Two more right turns and then a left, you'll come to our biggest exhibit. There's always three guys from security over that way."

She put her thumb under her metal nameplate and stuck it under Booker's nose. "You tell one of them that I sent you. Zora Berke. And they need to tell you where the bones' lab is—the one on five. How's that?"

"Couldn't be better, Ms. Berke," Booker said. "Thanks a bunch."

We were cruising in and around all the animals, following the guard's directions, until we turned a corner and I came to a complete stop.

Directly in front of me was the skeleton of the largest monster I'd ever seen. Its body filled a room the size of a football field, but its long neck didn't even fit within those walls. Instead, it hung out into the hallway, its fierce-looking face—with deep hollow spaces where its eyes should have been and a jaw as wide as my bed was long—hovering just over my head.

"What is it?" I asked, grabbing Booker's arm.

"You haven't seen it before? It's one of the newest exhibits here," Booker said. "It's called a Titanosaur, Dev. It's the largest creature that ever walked on earth."

17

"Mission accomplished," I said.

I was circling the Titanosaur, walking around his enormous display space, craning my neck so far back that it hurt, in order to look up at all the parts of his reconstructed body.

"You mean we're not going to keep hunting for the fossil lab today?" Booker asked.

"Of course we are. I mean I had to find a place for Mrs. Cion to tell the museum where to set up the cots for Katie's party," I said, "and this is going to be the spot. I promised her I'd do that."

"You nailed it."

"How come I don't know about this guy? This Titanosaur?"

"Your summer school project took you to the library, and mine brought me here," Booker said.

I stopped behind a group of people who were in front of one of the stands, reading the information that described the dinosaur and how it was found.

"You don't need to do that, Dev," Booker said.

"But I want to know all about it."

"I can tell you most of it," he said.

"Go on."

"There was this farmer in a really remote part of South America, who was riding on horseback to look for his lost sheep. Instead, he stumbled on this gigantic fossil—a leg bone that was taller than he was."

"Sounds like something that could happen in Montana," I said. "Where in South America did he live?"

"Patagonia. The part of Patagonia that's Argen—"

"*What?* Are you sure?"

"Of course I'm sure. Why are you talking so loud?"

"Sorry. I'm just surprised, is all."

"Why?"

"Because when Katie and I were doing our research at the Puzzle Palace on Monday, it turns out that the man who led the dig in Montana—Steve Paulson—had worked in Patagonia. Katie and I argued whether that was in Argentina or in Chile."

"You're both right," Booker said. "What did this Paulson guy do there?"

"I have no idea," I said, "but it's possible he was working on the dinosaur dig of this Titanosaur. I mean, that's what he does. And also, he was terminated."

"Why?"

I flipped the cover of my iPad closed. "Gotta find that out, Booker. Might be he was fired for doing something bad."

"Could be the dig ended when they got all the bones out of the ground."

"You're thinking just like Katie," I said. "And I'm not sure that's such a good thing."

"You can't be suspicious of everybody, Dev."

"Good point. I just like to be loaded with information."

Booker was marching straight to the first guard he saw, who was standing behind the giant left rear leg of the Titanosaur, urging some kids not to touch the exhibit.

"I was sent to talk to you by the nice lady over near the vertebrate section," Booker said. "We dropped by to see a friend of ours who just came to town."

"Yeah?"

"She's in the fossil lab. Her name is Ling Soo," Booker said. "She invited us to come up for just a few minutes."

"But we can't find it," I said.

"We've got fossils just about everywhere," the man said. "Take your pick."

"Upstairs," Booker said, pretty emphatically. "Like in one of the turrets."

The guard hesitated for a minute.

"Miss Berke," Booker said, "Zora Berke. She told us to come ask you."

"Oh, you know Zora?" the guard asked.

We do now, I thought to myself, nodding at him.

Booker smiled and said, "Yes, sir."

"You're talking about those people who just came in from Montana this week?" the guard asked.

"Exactly," I said.

"Well, then, you go out past the head and neck of Titanosaur and hang a left at his jawbone. After you see a water fountain, you'll come to a stairwell that's narrower than the others, that's got a blue velvet rope blocking it off," he said. "Go up those stairs, and Miss Soo and the team should be up there." He turned his attention back to the kids who were scrambling around the room.

"May I give your name to the next guard?" Booker asked. He was always so polite and so professional.

"You won't need my name, son. There aren't any guards upstairs—just staff. Our researchers know better than to rattle any of the bones."

We'd caught a real break. There wouldn't have to be security guards on duty in the museum labs. The only people allowed up there were trusted employees or paleontologists working with them.

We found the staircase and this time I ran up ahead of Booker. This turret was in a really old part of the museum that hadn't been renovated—not spiffy like the display areas that had got all the public attention. The paint on the walls was yellowed and chipped, and the dim lights overhead were just bare bulbs.

"Now what?" Booker asked, when we reached the landing.

It was completely empty, except for cushioned seats all around the sides. Big bay windows opened out from the turret, and I could see way north into Central Park.

Hallways stretched away in two opposite directions. We chose one and started walking along the corridor. There were cases lining the walls, reaching almost to the ceiling. They each held the bones of animals that had lived a very long time ago.

"Spooky," Booker said.

Two guys about Ling's age, dressed in jeans and T-shirts, were coming our way. Neither paid us any attention.

Three more older men, deep in conversation, passed us from behind. "Looking for someone?" one turned to ask.

"I'm a friend of the crew from Montana who brought in the new specimens this week," I said. "Just doing a quick 'hello.'"

"It's one of these rooms off to the left," the man said. "Ask anyone you see for what you need, miss."

At the first doorway, I stopped and looked inside. It was a lab of some sort, but the three people inside were studying small specimens of some sort under microscopes. It didn't seem to be work that related to dinosaurs.

Two or three doorways later, we struck gold.

"That's it, Booker!" I said, again too loud for his taste. "That's the Ditch!"

"What do you mean?"

"The clutch of eggs that Katie found," I said. "She named it the Ditch."

The giant mound, still mostly covered in plaster—but with the tops of three of the eggs already exposed—was sitting on top of a long worktable. There was a large pickax—to break up the plaster of Paris, I guessed—right next to it.

I started to tiptoe into the room. "You've got to check

this out, Booker. It's the most incredible thing I've ever seen, next to the Titanosaur."

Booker came into the lab and stood beside me, our heads bent over the eggs.

"I mean, I wasn't even ten feet away from Katie when she—"

"Get away from there!" A man's voice boomed at us from behind. "Who are you?" he asked. "Who let you in here?"

18

I almost fell against the table from the shock of someone cornering us in a strange place—even though this time we were the trespassers. I grabbed on to the edge of the table and steadied myself to look at the speaker, who had sneaked up on us—or so it seemed to me.

I turned my head to answer him.

"Mr. Paulson!" I said. "Steve!"

"Why, Dev. What are you doing up here?" The expression on his face went from clamped to relaxed in a split second.

"I—um—my mom and I saw you all on the news last night," I said, trying to control my stammer. "I was so excited that I brought my friend Booker to come say hi to you and your team. To—um—congratulate you on all the big news."

"I don't know how you got upstairs here, Dev. You're lucky no one called the police on you."

Steve didn't seem to realize that Booker Dibble and I

practically were the police in this city. I guess he didn't know about my mom's job.

"The security guard let us up," I said. "We only wanted to come for a few minutes."

"We didn't mean any harm," Booker added.

"I was only hoping to show Booker some of the fossils—like the ones Katie found on the dig, and Ling's teeth, from the duckbill," I said. "And maybe now that you're here, you can show us what this breaking-news-feathered-stuff is all about."

Steve put his hands on his hips, looked at the floor, and shook his head from side to side.

"Sneak preview, Steve?" I added, trying to mimic Booker's most sincere smile.

"I wish I could, Dev. But I gave Chip and Ling the day off, so I'm not even sure where things are stored yet."

"I'm really good at figuring out puzzles," I said, my eyes darting from shelf to shelf around the musty room. I was tempted to tell him about some of the other cases I'd solved. "Like where somebody might have put something valuable."

"If I remember correctly," Steve said, "the last time you and your pals got nosy, Dev, you wound up in a mud pile up to your neck."

I could have sworn there was a touch of menace in his voice, but my mother would challenge me to prove that.

"Well, it's really dry up here, Steve," I said. "Bone dry. Nothing to worry about in this museum."

"I'll tell you what, young lady," Steve said, rubbing his hands together. "Why don't you give us a few days to settle in and sort out the work ahead of us. This museum holds us to pretty strict standards."

"I understand that," Booker said, trying to move me along. "It makes sense."

"Middle of next week, get in touch with me—do you have my cell?—and we can try to plan a visit."

"That's okay, Steve," I said. "Ling gave me her contact information. I'll just text her. I wouldn't want to bother you."

"Ling won't be here much, Dev," Steve said. "You should have my e-mail."

"Why won't she?" I asked, surprised. "Doesn't she get to name her species and all that? I wouldn't leave my fossils alone for a minute, if I'd found any."

"Ling's got some serious work to do first," he said, stepping aside to usher Booker and me out of the lab. "She's got to write up our findings and have all the specimens and photographs validated, too."

"Why doesn't she do that right here?" I asked,

passing by him to get to the door. "At the museum, where they are."

"Actually, Ling has gone back to school. She's going to work with a group of experts at Yale," Steve said. "There's a lot of pressure on our team to make sure Ling gets this right. I'll be sending her pictures and information about everything she needs."

My head was spinning. Ling had withdrawn from Yale. I saw that fact with my own eyes when Katie and I looked her up on the program on the NYPD computer system.

"But—but Ling doesn't go to school at Yale anymore."

"Where in the world did you hear that, Dev?" Steve said, taking a step in my direction. "I don't know where you get your information young lady, but it's wrong."

"Dev must be mistaken, sir," Booker said, nudging me to move along.

"Yeah. Booker's right," I said, anxious to get on my way. "I must be confused with one of the other students I met."

"Don't go spreading unfounded rumors, Dev," Steve said. "You just stay away from Ling till I tell you she's done with her work."

19

"What do you make of that, Dev?" Booker asked. "I thought you said Steve was such a nice guy."

I was sitting on a bench with Booker outside the museum, winded from fleeing the lab. I think it was a combination of fear and flight.

"I've got to think it all through," I said. "Steve *is* a really nice guy, or he was. Maybe he's just under a lot of pressure. But where could Ling be?"

"And why did he tell you to keep away from Ling?" he asked. "We should call Yale and see what they tell us."

"That won't work. There are laws—some kind of privacy thing—that forbid colleges and universities from giving out information about their students."

"How about if I take another shot at my undercover scholar role? It was a big hit at the library."

"Booker Dibble—kid paleontologist?"

"You and Katie were just on a dig last week."

"Not as scholars, Booker. We were there as volunteer tagalongs."

"Mozart wrote his first composition when he was

five, Dev," Booker said, standing straighter and pulling himself up to full height. "I know a couple of guys at Yale who graduated from Hunter."

"Yeah, but what do you know about dinosaurs?"

"The Titanosaur, Miss Quick, is roughly the size of ten large elephants."

"That's not scientific, Booker. That's obvious."

"Maybe it's time to consult the commissioner on this matter, don't you think?" Booker asked.

"The commissioner likes it best when detectives present themselves with complete case files," I said. "Let's take the weekend to put all our facts together, and then—ugh, I'll admit it—we might want to ask for her help."

My phone buzzed in my jeans' pocket.

"I think I've left five messages for you already," Katie said. "How come you're not picking up?"

"I had no idea you'd called. You know these old buildings in New York," I said, clamping my hand to my mouth before I let my whereabouts slip to Katie. "I mean, that staircase up to the crown in the Statue of Liberty? You've been there. There's no reception whatsoever. It's so old and the walls are so thick."

"Well, I spoke to Kyle," Katie said. "I think he really misses us—well, me especially."

“That should make you happy,” I said. “What else do you know?”

“I’ll start with the tire tracks. Turns out the Road Warrior model is all over town,” Katie said. “There’s an Atlas dealer in Big Timber, and the machines are way cheaper than the John Deere tractors. There must be two or three hundred of them in and around my dad’s ranch. That makes it so much harder for us, don’t you think?”

“It makes it so much harder for *Kyle*,” I said. “We’ve got enough to do on our end.”

“What’s his assignment?” Katie asked. “He and I are going to FaceTime later tonight.”

“Cool,” I said, shaking my head at Katie’s puppy love. “I’ll forward the photographs I took of the tire tracks last week. When he finds an Atlas, he’ll have to see whether or not the tread is worn out in places, like it seems to be in my pictures.”

Katie didn’t say anything.

“Are you still there?” I asked.

“Yeah,” Katie said. “I need to tell you something, but you can’t go deducing anything from it, okay? Will you promise?”

“I won’t jump to any conclusions, if that’s what you mean. Deducing, however, is like second nature to me.”

"Maybe I shouldn't—"

"C'mon, Katie. Every little factoid helps."

"Well, Kyle's dad has an Atlas Road Warrior," she said as softly as she could speak. "You met Mr. Lowry. You know he didn't drive it onto the hillside during the night. You just know that."

This wasn't the moment to ask Katie if Kyle's dad had an alibi. This was a time to trust the people we knew and liked.

"I'm really glad you told me," I said. "The Lowrys are our friends. You can tell Kyle to relax. And that his dad's tractor might be a good place for him to practice, just to see if there's a difference in the tread marks the tractor makes in his own driveway and the ones I photographed. You sure you're not upset?"

"Thanks, Dev. I feel better just saying it out loud."

Even with Kyle searching, I wasn't hopeful. I had no idea how we could find our Road Warrior among two hundred of them, like a needle in a haystack that was known as Big Timber. "Did you find anything out about Chip?"

"There are Donners all over Sweet Grass County," Katie said. "Some are related to one another and some are just out there on their own."

"What does Kyle know about Chip?"

"Nothing yet. We can't even figure out which one he is," Katie said.

"I don't know what you mean."

"In the county phone directory, Dev, there are four Donners whose first name begins with the letter C," Katie said. "There's Charles A. Donner, and Charles Q. Donner, and Charlton Donner, and Chester, too."

"Hard to tell which one of those might have Chip as a nickname, I guess. I was hoping there would just be a plain old Chip or Chipper."

"There is a Chipper, Dev. But she's a woman," Katie said. "Not our guy."

I pulled my steno pad out of my rear pocket and wrote down the four names Kyle had given her. "Good job, Katie. Tell Kyle I'll e-mail these over to Sergeant Tapply so he can do a background check on each of them."

"I hope they're good clues," she said. "What are you and Booker doing now?"

I had to keep up the pretense that Booker and I had gone to the Statue of Liberty and not the museum. "You know how long that ferry ride from Liberty Island takes, Katie. I'll talk to you later. Thanks for this."

"Let's walk through the park," Booker said. "Grab some ice cream."

"Give me a sec to call Tapp, okay?"

I dialed the number and Tapp answered. "What's up, Dev?"

"I've got some names for you. Would you mind running them through CLEAR?"

"I promised you that much, didn't I?" Sergeant Tapply asked me. "You're not making an arrest without clearing it with the commissioner, are you?"

"These four guys live in Montana. I mean, I know about the long arm of the law, Tapp, but even if my mom deputizes us, Booker's arm won't stretch that far," I said. "It's all just background."

"Let me have 'em," he said.

I read off the names of the four Donner men and told Tapp that was all I knew about them. Not their ages or occupations or any other stats.

"I'll be back to you later, Dev."

"Thanks, Tapp."

Booker and I walked into the park, bought two ice-cream cones at the entrance, and started winding our way on the footpath until we arrived at the lake. The ice cream we got was dripping down the sides of our cones nonstop.

We rented a rowboat and glided around, under Bow Bridge and up to the far corner of the lake—Booker manning the oars, letting me hang my feet over the edge into the water, warning me about the approach of snapping turtles as they came up to catch the afternoon sun.

I couldn't believe more than half the summer had flown by. Booker was going on about his fall classes, but I was thinking about fossils I'd always done some of my best thinking on rowboat lake.

After a lazy hour, we returned the boat to the attendant, I put my sneakers back on, and we were about to split up—Booker to go west to his home, and me to the east to mine—when my phone rang.

"Dev?"

"Yeah."

"It's me. Tapp. I think I found your man," he said. "You're just looking to credit this guy in Katie's essay, right?"

"That's what we had in mind."

"Well, it's not Charlie A. or Charlie Q. Donner," Tapp said. "And it's not Chester, either. But Charlton's got himself an aka, Dev."

"An aka? What's that?"

"Sorry. It's cop talk for 'also known as,' like an alias. And Charlton Donner's alias is Chip."

"That's so helpful, Tapp. Maybe you've got a home address and a phone number, too," I said. "That would really save our friend Kyle some time."

"I got all that, Dev," he said. "But I've also got some news that might interest you to know."

"Shoot, Tapp."

"Chip Donner must know the sheriff pretty well. He seems to have spent some time in the Sweet Grass County jail."

"What?" I shrieked, grabbing Booker's elbow as hard as I could. "What was he arrested for?"

"It looks like he got a little disorderly with folks at a local event three years ago," Tapp said. "Might have been some rowdy fans at a football game, from the location of occurrence. But the charges against him were dismissed."

Chip Donner was a large man. I wouldn't want any guy I knew to be on the other side of any kind of a problem with him.

"That's good," I said.

Disorderly conduct didn't signal any kind of dishonesty, as my mother had told me often. It could have been an attack of some sort—which would have been bad—or it could have been a matter of self-defense, like Tapp suggested.

"I owe you, Sergeant Tapply," I said. "I'm baking cupcakes with Natasha tomorrow. I'll see you get a batch of them on Monday."

"Hold on there, Dev," Tapp said. "Don't you want to know the rest?"

"There's more?"

"Chip Donner has an open case pending in Sweet Grass County."

"What's the charge?" I asked, holding my breath.

"Grand Larceny in the Third Degree," Tapp said.

"He stole something?" I asked. "Chip Donner's a thief?"

"Nothing's been proved yet," Tapp said. "I've got to remind you of that."

"Well, what's he accused of?"

"It says here he stole a vehicle. That's all that's in the public record."

"But we've got to know, Tapp," I said. "Is he a car thief, or is it something else?"

"I'm looking it over again, Dev. The fact that it's third degree means the value of the vehicle was pretty cheap," Tapp said. "It could have been a car if it's an old one, or a used one, without a lot of value."

"I guess it could have been a small tractor, too," I said, leaving deductions in the dirt and leapfrogging to conclusions. "Some of them are cheaper than cars. What if Chip Donner stole a Road Warrior?"

20

"What a nice surprise," my mother said to Booker, when she and Sam came through the door at six thirty that evening. "Did Dev bring you home to rope you into walking the dog for her?"

"Hey, Aunt Blaine," Booker said, kissing her on the cheek, before he went in for a one-armed hug with Sam "I was planning to go home but—"

"It's more serious than that, Mom," I said. "I had to stop Booker from going back across the park to get home for dinner. And yes, Asta's been fed and walked."

"Then what's so serious?" she asked, dropping her tote bag full of case reports and police files on the floor in the dining room, where she used the table as her office. "Sam's making his famous burgers for dinner, Booker. I'll call your mother. You can stay and eat with us."

"I need to update you on the Montana investigation," I said. "Can we all sit down in the living room? I think we need your help."

Asta practically attached herself to my mother's side

until she sat on the sofa and scratched the dog behind both ears.

"There is no investigation in Big Timber, Dev," my mother said. "Case closed. I thought you understood that."

"I've been doing a little more digging."

"Have you hit another mudflat, dear?" she asked.

My mother slipped out of her high heels and put her feet up on the sofa. Sam was getting us all something to drink.

"Nope. My neck is still above the muck," I said. "So I asked Tapp to run some names for us through the CLEAR program."

"Fortunately, that man has very few secrets from me. Go ahead."

"Here's where we need your help."

"'We?' Have you dragged Booker into this one, too?" my mother asked. "I thought you two were going to the museum to pick out a spot for the party."

"Did all that, Mom. I called Mrs. Cion and she's very appreciative."

"So Booker's here because—?"

"Because you have so much more respect for his judgment than you have for mine. Well, sometimes you do."

"I have great respect for your sense of justice and for

your doggedness and for your enthusiasm, darling. It's just sometimes your instincts mislead you," my mother said. "And mislead Booker. And mislead Katie. What is it you want me to do?"

I started to explain what the name check on Chip had turned up, but my mother's reaction was flat.

"You just don't know enough to be distrusting him and everyone who was on that hillside, Dev," she said.

Sam came back into the room with their drinks. "You know your mother isn't from the 'where there's smoke, there's bound to be fire' school of prosecution. She likes hard proof before she accuses anyone of a crime. That's part of what makes her good at what she does—part of what gives her credibility."

"I get that, Sam," I said, "but how about where there's not only smoke, but there are actually sparks—sparks that could turn into flames at a moment's notice."

"Show me a spark, Dev," my mother said.

I was sitting on the living room floor. I reached up to the mug on the coffee table and grabbed a handful of pencils.

"Here's Steve Paulson," I said, laying a pencil on the carpet. "He had a job in Patagonia not too long ago—maybe on a dig there—"

"Maybe," my mother said, slowly and with emphasis.

"And he was terminated."

"In which meaning of that word?" she asked. "Did the job he was doing reach an end? Was he fired? Did the entire project just terminate?"

"I don't know, Mom," I said, pursing my lips. I had seen her cross-examine the smartest experts and reduce them to an endless list of 'I don't knows' in a courtroom. It wasn't pretty.

"Do you want me to ask him why?" she asked.

I held out my arm. "Not yet, but thanks. Please listen to me like you would to a grown-up, okay? I'm really aiming to be methodical."

She took a sip of her white wine.

"Then you have Ling Soo, who told Katie and me she was a grad student at Yale." I put the second pencil down, placing it across the first one—touching it, but going in another direction.

"But she's not, Aunt Blaine," Booker said. "Sergeant Tapply said the system shows that she's withdrawn from the university."

"And yet Steve says she's still there," I said. "Both can't be true."

"When did he tell you that?" Sam asked.

I sat straight up. That had been a sloppy slip on my part, admitting I had talked to Steve.

"Um—today—at the museum," I said. "Booker and I ran into him."

My mother rested her head back on the pillow behind her and closed her eyes. Stories about how I conducted my investigations often had that effect on her.

"That's a bit of luck in a museum half the size of Rhode Island," Sam said.

"To be honest—"

"I hope you're always honest, dear," my mother said, still in her "I'm-not-sure-I-want-to-hear-what-comes-out-of-your-mouth-next" kind of mood.

"Of course, Mom. I mean as soon as Booker and I settled on a place for Katie's slumber party this afternoon, I thought I'd check whether Ling was around and say hi. You know, after the news story last night, I figured there was a good chance she might be at the museum."

"If you're a dino guru, you go where the dinos are," Sam said.

"Exactly my point, Sam."

"So where did you run into Steve?" Sam asked. "At the T. rex or the Triceratops?"

"The guard let us go to the office where our team from Montana is working," I said.

"Promise me, Booker Dibble," my mother said, holding the cold glass of wine against her forehead, "that you both had better sense than to climb down into one of those dungeon-like stairwells to look for these people. I count on you being the brakes on Dev's gusto."

"No basements, Aunt Blaine," Booker said. "We kind of bumped right into Steve in the workspace the paleontologists use. It's upstairs, not down."

"That's when Steve told us Ling was back at school."

My mother opened her eyes and sat up to take another sip of wine. "Could be she enrolled in classes again. Ling's obviously a very smart young woman."

"Now let me give you the third piece of news," I said, "that Booker and I just got from Tapp on my way home."

"I hope you've done nothing that will spoil my appetite, Dev," she said.

"It's not about me, Mom. It's Chip Donner," I said, stacking a third pencil on top of the others. "You know, he's the guy that made Katie give up her fossils the first night. And he even left the campsite that same night because his wife was sick at home."

That was another good piece of circumstantial evidence.

"Yes, Chip Donner," my mother said, chiding me a bit. "The really nice man who laid down on the ground and held on to you for dear life so you didn't sink any deeper in the mud. I'm familiar with his name."

"He's got an arrest record, Mom. A rap sheet, with two collars."

"You've got my lingo down to perfection, Devlin Quick," Sam said. "Don't let your grandmother hear you talking like that."

"Too late, Sam. Lulu wants a gold shield, too."

"Arrested for what?" my mother asked.

"An assault," I said. "No weapon involved. A fight with someone at a football stadium that was dismissed. But the second case is still pending."

"Tell me about it," she said.

"Chip Donner stole something, Mom. A vehicle of some sort. Not a fancy one," I said. "Because Tapp said the level of the crime is based on the value of the thing that was stolen, and this is only third degree."

She was taking me more seriously now. She put the wineglass on the table and leaned in, steepling the fingers of her hands. "You're thinking of some kind of tractor or compact dozer like the one that left tracks on the dig site last week?"

"I can't call Sheriff Brackley, Mom. I know he won't give me any information without checking with Sam or you first," I said. "That's why I need your help."

"That's an easy call to make, Dev. I'll do it while Sam's getting dinner ready," she said. "And I'm grateful that you've come to me, instead of going out of control and doing things you shouldn't be doing."

"You're the best, Mom!" I said, reaching out to squeeze her hand.

She straightened out her legs to get up. "I don't get the point of your pickup sticks," she said, pointing at the pile of pencils on the floor. "You better put them away before one of us slips on them, Dev."

"They're not pickup sticks, Mom. I want you to think of them as logs at a campsite. Put a match to each one of them—Steve or Ling or Chip—and I'd bet anything there'd be more than smoke and sparks," I said. "I know how serious it is to say someone is guilty or innocent—"

"You're right about that," my mom said, leaning over to look at my little pile of logs.

"If you rub these three together," I said, thinking of Steve and Ling and Chip, "I bet we'd be looking at a full-on fire."

21

"Still no sign of fire," my mother said, standing behind me at the front door, as we said good night to our company at nine o'clock. Sam was going upstate for the weekend and he agreed to give Booker a ride home. "We'll all just have to relax and wait for the sheriff to return my call."

"That's a good thing," Sam said, looking at me. "I'm off-duty for the weekend. You need to give your brain a rest, Dev. Just enjoy Katie's party."

"Will do."

I actually liked it best when my brain was on overdrive. Sleuthing could keep me going 24/7, if my mom didn't put a lid on it.

She had called Sheriff Brackley's office and left him a message. Apparently, the top dog in every police department didn't have a Sergeant Tapply by his side to take care of business when he was away from his desk.

Booker held up his hand to me in a wave. "Tomorrow, Dev. See you on the way to the party."

"Bye, guys," I said.

"I've got some homework to do," my mother said, turning to me after she closed the door. "Are you going to read, or watch TV?"

"Read, probably," I said, kissing her on the cheek and heading back to my room.

I washed up and got into bed, checking my laptop for e-mails. It was only an hour later in Buenos Aires, Argentina, where Liza de Lucena lived, than it was in New York. Maybe she'd be up to Skyping with me.

I popped her a text. "Miss you," I said, which was true. "Can you talk?"

Liza replied right away. "Yes! Want to Skype?"

"You bet. I'll start it up."

I hadn't spoken to Liza since I'd gone to Montana with Katie. She lived with her family in Buenos Aires, where both of her parents were schoolteachers, and she had won a scholarship for the Ditchley summer program. Liza lived at our home and we had instantly hit it off together during our first investigation.

"Hey, Liza. It's so good to see you."

She was smiling widely, still sporting her braces.

"*Como esta?*" I asked her. "I'm practicing my Spanish so I can come visit you someday."

"That would be so cool," Liza said. "How's your mom? And Natasha?"

"They're good. But the house is too quiet without you, and even Asta keeps sniffing around your bed, trying to find your scent."

"*Gracias,* Dev," she said. "And how is Booker?"

"He's fine." I didn't dare tell her he had just left the apartment, and that I hadn't thought to include him on the Skype.

These girls and their crushes were just something I didn't entirely understand. I needed to get my mother settled into a relationship. Then maybe I could turn my attention to boys.

"How was Montana?"

"It was amazing," I said, launching into my description of Big Sky Country and the Badlands—and of course, the dino dig and all the curious events surrounding it.

"I think adventure finds *you*, Dev. You're like a magnet for mystery," Liza said.

"Sam will like that turn of phrase."

"Maybe when I come back to New York, your force field will draw me into some excitement."

"You know, Liza, you don't even have to wait that long," I said, getting right to the point. "Have you ever been to Patagonia?"

"No. Why?"

"Well, have you ever heard of a dinosaur called the Titanosaur?"

"Of course I have! Those fossils were found in *La Flecha*, which is like our desert."

"You've got to see this creature, Liza. He's on display now at the Museum of Natural History. You have to come back here."

"I hope my parents can travel with me next time. You know my mother teaches science at the high school," Liza said. "That's all her students could talk about when *Il Titanosaur* was found."

"Actually," I said, "I was hoping that your mom might know someone who worked on the dig."

"She would have told me if she did, Dev."

"Oh, that's too bad." I tried to hide the disappointment in my voice, but I suspect Liza saw my expression.

"But I know she has friends at the museum here, where those fossils were on display before they moved to New York," Liza said. "At the *Museo Paleontológico* in Patagonia."

"That's exactly what I need, Liza," I said. "A connection to a paleontologist in your country."

"What for?"

"Well, how did your mom feel about our investigation last month? Does she know how brave you are?"

Liza hesitated before she answered. "She's very proud of me for getting the award from the mayor, but she really didn't want my father to know all the details."

I grimaced.

"I think she was just being protective of me, Dev. Not disapproving."

"Do you think she would help me?"

"I'm sure she would," Liza said. "What do you want her to do?"

"I'd like her to talk to one of the paleontologists—you know, just a phone call," I said. "I'd like her to ask around about an American named Steve Paulson, who might have been part of the team that dug up the Titanosaur."

Liza was slow to answer. "It's not dangerous or anything like that for my mother to get involved?"

"I'd never ask her to do anything that would put her in harm's way, Liza."

My mother faced down the city's worst criminals every day that she was on the job, but not everybody could be this way.

"What then?"

"Just to find out whether Steve was involved, and if so, exactly what his job was," I said. "And why he was terminated."

“What will you do with the information? If my mother can get any,” Liza asked.

“My mom might talk it over with the sheriff in Montana, if yours gets any interesting news,” I said. “Or President Sutton, the head of our museum, might want to know about it.”

“Do you think this Steve Paulson is a bad guy?” Liza asked.

“My opinion counts for very little in all this,” I said, calling up words my mother had spoken often over the years. “I’m looking for facts, Liza. Nothing but the facts.”

22

"Could you all cut down on the giggles?" Booker asked.

It was almost six o'clock on Saturday evening. Mrs. Cion had hired a van to pick each of the kids up, and the last would be Katie.

Booker and three of our friends—Tanya, Amy, and Rachel—were already on board when the van stopped for Natasha and me. We had all been instructed to bring sleeping bags to place on top of the cots provided by the museum, and our pajamas and toothbrushes.

Natasha had baked three dozen chocolate cupcakes this morning—a dozen for Tapp—and I had frosted them. Then I squiggled Katie's name in pink and turquoise letters on top, drawing bones and dino eggs—and on one, a tiny heart for Kyle Lowry.

"How's this going to be a surprise anyway?" Rachel asked.

"When we get to Katie's building," Natasha said, "Mrs. Cion is going to blindfold her and bring her down to the van. That way, she won't know where she's going till we get in the door of the museum."

The squealing started again.

Booker was in the back row of seats. "Amy, you're going to shatter the glass in every window of this thing with that voice of yours."

"She's been this way since pre-K," Tanya said. "You know that. You started out with us in the same school."

"Is there time for me to rethink spending Saturday night with all of you?" Booker asked.

"No chance," I said.

Katie was in the lobby of her building, and I could see Mrs. Cion had tied a red and black bandanna around her head. Then they walked out to the van and Natasha helped Katie step up, while the driver threw her sleeping bag in the rear.

"Have a great time, kids," Mrs. Cion called out, waving us off. "I can't believe you're officially twelve!"

It only took ten minutes to get to the museum entrance on West Seventy-Seventh Street.

There was a guard on the door, who laughed along with us as we guided Katie down the ramp and through the doors.

"Any idea where you are?" Rachel asked.

"No way," Katie said. "I'm stumped."

She was probably hoping she was on the ground floor of a fancy jewelry store, free to roam around and pick out some trinkets. But the most interesting museum in the world would have to do.

"Ready?" Booker asked. "I'm going to take off your blindfold."

Katie could hardly stand still. Her feet were dancing in place and her fists were pumping up and down. Booker stood behind her and untied the knot in the bandanna.

Katie blinked her eyes and looked up. "I don't believe it! It's the Great Canoe," she said, standing right below the carved killer whale on its prow. "We're in the museum. My party's in the museum!"

"Are you okay with that, Katie?" I asked. I felt a little bit guilty having steered Mrs. Cion to this location, mostly because I wanted to be here myself. I had hoped Katie's colossal find in Montana had fueled the spirit of adventure in her.

"Totally! This is so cool, Dev!"

"Okay, kids," a twenty-something-year-old African American woman tried to get our attention. "My name is Keisha, and I'm going to be your guide for the night."

All of us stopped chattering and listened up.

"First thing I do is give each one of you an ID card

to keep around your neck on this lanyard," she said, passing out long yellow cords with the museum's logo on them. "Then you each get a mini-flashlight, because the museum is closed to everyone but you all tonight, and some of these hallways get pretty dark."

There were a few ohs and ahs from our pals.

Then Keisha addressed Katie directly. "You're the birthday girl, right?"

Katie bounced a bit. "I am."

"Well, your friends have picked out a special place for you to spend the night," Keisha said. "Any idea where that might be?"

Katie pointed her finger, first at me and then at Booker, laughing as she did. "I didn't believe for a minute that you were going to the Statue of Liberty yesterday!"

"Fiblet, Katie," I said, crossing my heart. "But in a really good cause."

"Somewhere in the museum that has something to do with dinosaurs, right?" Katie said.

"You'll be sleeping next to the biggest one ever," Keisha answered. "So if you all pick up your bags and things, we'll take the elevator to the fourth floor, and I'll introduce you to the Titanosaur. He'll be your bedtime companion tonight."

We piled into the elevator and took it up to four. The first thing Katie saw, from the end of the building that was our approach, was the elongated neck of the giant creature snaking out of the exhibition room and into the hallway.

"He's looking for me, you guys!" she shouted.

It was as though the ancient animal was craning his neck to find a friend in the quiet corridor, trying to escape from the space where he was penned in.

On both sides of his enormous body, cots had been set up for our group.

"Here's what you do," Keisha said. "Pick your place and plop down your sleeping bags. We're going to go to the food court, where you'll have your dinner. Then I'll give you a flashlight walking tour of the museum before I say good night."

"I want to be in the middle of all of you," Katie said, throwing her bag on a cot right beside the belly of the beast.

"I need to be outside of squeal-central," Booker said, choosing one of the first two cots that was halfway out in the corridor, beneath the dino's neck.

"I'll be opposite Booker," I said.

"You've got to be closer to me, Dev," Katie said.

"Hey, I had you all to myself in Montana," I said.

"Don't you want one of the other girls to have a turn?"

"Good idea," Katie said.

Booker looked at me and nodded.

Natasha took her stuff—and a thick book to read—and went to the farthest end, near the Titanosaur's tail. We all threw our things down and followed Keisha to the closest food court.

Dinner was hot dogs and chips, and when it came time for dessert, Natasha surprised Katie with the platter of cupcakes, all aglow with lighted candles. We sang "Happy Birthday" and Katie beamed with delight.

"Whose idea was this?" she leaned over and whispered to me.

"It was a combination of me and your mom," I said. "She talked to me about it when we were at the rodeo our last night in Montana, and because of the dig, I thought it would be extra special. It's kind of perfect, isn't it?

Katie squeezed my hand. "This is just a really cool place to celebrate. Especially since I got permission to keep the bones I dug up."

Lulu had a phrase for my modesty in this kind of situation. Something Latin that meant don't hog all the cred when it isn't necessary.

Each of us had a gift for our friend—a wallet, some hair accessories, books, and a diary from Natasha.

I had gone shopping with my mother earlier in the day and gave Katie a small box. "It's not real gold, Katie," I said, "but it's something you wanted."

She ripped off the paper and opened the lid. In it was a locket on a chain—which would have to do until her parents sprung for something better—since I had distracted them from the gift Katie wanted most. I had downloaded and cut up a photo of Kyle in his rodeo gear to put inside the locket.

"I love you, Dev," she said, putting the chain around her neck before she reached over and hugged me tight. "Best birthday ever."

"Most excellent," Booker said. He got up and walked out of the food court. I could tell he was ready to get on with our business.

I walked out to catch up to him. "Just be patient a little longer," I said. "You've got to admit it's a really special opportunity to have this whole place to ourselves."

"I'm more interested in whether the sheriff got back to your mom about Chip Donner."

"Nope," I said. "She called again today but the outgoing voice mail in his office said he won't be back until Monday. I guess there isn't a lot of crime in Big Timber."

"How about Liza?" he asked.

"You should Skype with her yourself, Booker. She likes you a lot."

He put his hands in his pockets and shrugged. "Yeah. You're not kidding about that. Did her mother make the call to the museum people in Patagonia about Steve?"

"Not yet, so far as I can tell. But it's not so urgent," I said. "We've got our own work to do."

"Maybe we should just let sleeping bones lie, Dev," Booker said.

"That's sleeping dogs, you mean, Booker. Not dinos," I said. "We'll see if these bones can tell tales."

23

"This is called the rotunda," Keisha said as we all gathered around her in the entrance hall of the museum. "You probably know that this area and the halls beyond are a memorial to Theodore Roosevelt."

I looked up at the painted canvas murals on the walls—covered with zebras, lions, antelopes, and other exotic animals. There were vibrant paintings of Genghis Khan and other explorers, panels filled with early surveying equipment and with scientists conducting research experiments. And always back to Teddy Roosevelt—here, posed with the long guns he used to hunt wildlife in Africa in 1909, and there his role in the digging of the Panama Canal.

"Not only was TR a statesman and scholar, a great conservationist and historian," Keisha said, "but this museum was really in his blood. Teddy's father was one of our founding trustees, and the museum's charter was signed in his father's home in 1869."

Keisha was moving us along, through the Hall of

African Mammals and down the stairs to the Hall of Ocean Life. As we walked, she explained the history of the collection and answered all our questions, no matter what they were about.

I had other plans for the night, but I had to admit to myself that this was a pretty amazing way to see the museum. Keisha was a wonderful storyteller and it was easy to be sucked in by her tales. So much had changed in the way people all over the world lived their lives and took care of the natural world.

Other than the backlighting in the dioramas and exhibition cases, the only glow in each hallway came from the flashlights that the eight of us were holding.

"I'd like you all to point your beams up at the whale," Keisha said. "He's a giant blue whale—which over the centuries has been hunted almost to extinction—but is still the largest animal alive today.

"This one is ninety-four feet long," Keisha said. "It was found off the coast of South America in 1925."

I'd seen this one so many times I could recite the numbers myself.

"What are you going to do about Natasha?" Booker was standing behind me, talking into my right ear.

"Not to worry," I said. "I asked Natasha for help with my summer math project last night."

"That's no joke, Dev. You really need it."

"No kidding," I said. "We didn't get started until after you and Sam left, and I kept her at it till eleven o'clock. That's when she went out to meet with her friends."

"Did she have a late night?"

"Let me just say that Natasha's cupcake moves were a little slow today," I said. "She told me she was out till after two this morning."

"She must have been really tired, Dev. You let her sleep late, right?"

"Not a chance, Booker. I was on her at dawn about baking for Katie."

Amy turned her head and told us to be quiet. Really, Amy? What is it about this old blue whale that every schoolkid in New York doesn't know?

"So if you want to see how the whale gets his bubble bath once every year," Keisha said, pointing up at the giant sea creature suspended overhead, "we live stream it, complete with soap suds, rubber gloves, ladders, and the longest-handled brooms you've ever seen."

We followed her to the elevator to get to the third floor.

"This place is so huge," I said to Keisha, when we were waiting in the corridor for everyone to catch up. "Is it scary to be here at night? Are the security guards going to be up on the fourth floor with us?"

Keisha patted my arm. "You'll all be fine. There's never been a problem here. During the night, the security guards are downstairs, watching the exits and entrances—because you're the only ones here. You just scamper on down if you think you've got a problem. Is that okay?"

"Yes, ma'am," I said. She had no idea just how okay that was for me and Booker.

Katie was so excited to be on a private tour with the museum all to ourselves that it was hard to push Keisha to move faster.

Natasha was yawning more regularly now. Her exhaustion was probably exaggerated by the darkness of the corridors and the low level of air-conditioning kept on at night.

The museum was stuffy and dark, and I was glad for that. Everyone would feel sleepy before too long.

We took one of the double-long staircases up to the fourth floor and the home of the Titanosaur.

"So, we're back at the Titanosaur, where we all started, almost two hours ago," Keisha said. "Are your feet aching?"

Natasha's "yes" spoke for all of us.

"Just a few things about this amazing specimen," Keisha said. "Then I'll point you down the hall to the restrooms, so you can change and get ready for bed."

Booker gave me a thumbs-up.

"How many of you know what a fossil is?" Keisha asked.

"An old bone," Rachel said. "I mean really old."

"That's a good start. But a fossil is really any evidence of prehistoric life—whether animal or plant—that's at least ten thousand years old," Keisha said. "Bones and teeth are the more common ones that we see, but there are fossils of footprints as well as skin impressions, too."

"They're called body fossils when they were part of an animal organism," Booker said, "and trace fossils if they're just about anything else, like footprints and stuff."

"You're right," Keisha said.

"He's not smarter than we are," I said, trying to make the girls laugh. "He's just super into science."

"I love science, too," Amy said. "The whole point of fossilization is that it turns bones into rocks."

"Exactly," Keisha said.

"You mean this whole giant skeleton that's hanging over me tonight," Katie said, "is made out of rock?"

"What if it falls down?" Rachel asked. "It will break every bone in my body. I'm going to move my cot farther away."

"Don't worry, girls," Keisha said. "Titanosaur is just a model, like most of the other dinos on display. He's been digitally remade—out of fiberglass—from the original fossils that were found in Argentina. Every detail is accurate, but it's just a replica."

"A replica?" It took a minute for me to absorb those words. "Made of fiberglass? You mean those aren't the real bones?"

"That's the way museums do things these days," Keisha said. "You'd never even know, would you?"

I could feel a sense of panic as my chest tightened.

"But where are the bones? I mean the fossils. The original fossils," I said. My anxiety was kicking in, wondering what would become of Katie's discoveries—her fossils and her clutch of eggs—and when they might disappear.

"I can't say that I'm sure exactly, at least not for each exhibit," Keisha said. "I know the museum keeps most of the real fossils for research, but some are stored here and lots are stored off-site."

"My mom says there are bones all over the place in this museum," Booker said. "Fossils, I mean, on shelves everywhere. Millions of them. Miles of them, actually."

Keisha scrunched up her face. "Is your mother a paleontologist?"

"Nope. She's an orthopedic surgeon," he said. "That's why bones fascinate her."

"Did she ever say where she saw them?" Keisha asked.

"There are pictures online," he said, "on the museum site. She showed them to me this week, because we were coming here."

Keisha shrugged. "They could be in one of the sub-basements, I guess," she said. "We've got miles and miles of things on shelves downstairs. I've never looked at all the specimens that are labeled, but I'm sure we can find someone to help you do that when you decide to come back."

"Can you take us to see some of them?" I asked, practically before she could finish the sentence. "Just a sampling?"

Natasha was on me in a flash. "This is enough for tonight, don't you think?"

"Anything else, before I let you go off to dream about all these wonderful treasures?" Keisha asked.

I had turned my back on the Titanosaur and was looking in a display case at some smaller fossils.

"Yes, please," I said. "One more thing. Do you know whether anyone tries to get any DNA off the fossil, on its outside?"

"Okay, so you don't mean inside the bones or rock?"

"No, ma'am. Just the outside," I said. "You know, like trace evidence? I've seen it done on crime scenes on TV shows."

"What would that tell you, Dev?" Keisha asked. "Explain to the others, please."

"Oh, like maybe who had touched the thing in the first place," I said.

"Not very likely," she said, shaking her head from side to side.

"Why not?"

"Take those bones from Katie's dig in Montana, which she was telling me about while we were just walking around tonight," Keisha said. "They were all encased in plaster of Paris in order to be shipped back here. The preparators—"

"The what?" I asked. The word sounded too close for comfort to perpetrators.

"Preparators," Keisha said.

I repeated both words quickly to myself, almost tripping over the similar syllables. "Who are they?"

"That's the name for the highly skilled technicians who work in labs, extracting the fossils from their plaster casts and working on all kinds of specimens," Keisha said. "They use adhesives and resins to make sure the samples stay safe. I would think there'd be no chance at all of finding DNA from diggers like Katie—because of all the handling that goes on—any more than I figure you'd be able to find fingerprints."

"I get it," I said, spinning the words around in my brain.

"The best information," Keisha said, "may lie deep inside those rocks. That's the snapshot we all wish we could get."

The other kids surrounded Keisha to thank her for making the evening so much fun.

Booker was just as bummed as I was. "Not the answer you were hoping for, Dev, was it?"

"Just think of it as a bump in the road," I said.

Natasha was helping each of the girls put their sleeping bags on top of their cots. I unfolded mine and grabbed my turquoise cotton pajamas and toothbrush.

"Men's room is the other way, Booker," I said.

"You still up for prowling around in the dark?" he asked, toothbrush in hand.

"You bet I am. We can just call it exercise, okay? It's good for us."

"How will you decide when?"

"Same as you," I said. "First, we'll let Katie enjoy every minute of her party. That's the most important thing. I know she wants to play charades for awhile, and I'm up for anything else that's fun for her."

"I'm in," Booker said.

"Sooner or later, the chatter will stop," I said, "and the girls will quiet down."

"And Natasha?" Booker asked. "What if she's still reading when our friends close their mouths?"

"I'll know," I said. "She makes noise when she sleeps."

"Natasha snores?" Booker asked, screwing up his nose.

"I wouldn't call it that. I say she snortles—short little snorts that are way cuter than snores."

"You'll hear Natasha, even on this end of the Titanosaur, out in the hallway here?"

"Atwells," I said, pointing to my ear with my free hand. "Generations of great auditory perception, Booker. I'll hear the lightest little snort, I promise."

"And staying awake?" he asked. "Can you manage that for yourself?"

"You bet," I said. "It's hard to fall asleep when you're reading Edgar Allan Poe."

"That's true," Booker said.

"And then there's our adventure that lies ahead," I said. "You and I have to get to the bottom of this. What if Katie's dino had a telltale heart?"

"You'd hear it beating, Dev, wherever it is. I'm sure of that."

24

Total darkness surrounded the Titanosaur in his lair.

Poe was always best read by flashlight, in the pitch-black of night for full effect, but it was also nice to be surrounded by my flock of friends as the beast hovered over me in the dark.

I saw Natasha's light go out, and I waited about five more minutes. Then she made that familiar snorting noise—it seemed loud enough to wake the T. rex in the rotunda, though it didn't disturb the Ditchley crew.

I reached over and wiggled Booker's big toe. No response. I grabbed all five toes of his left foot and pulled on them.

He propped himself up on one arm and shook his head until he focused on my face.

I stood up, put on my slippers, and signaled to Booker to follow me. He did. There is nothing in the world better than a best friend who rises to the occasion every single time.

We followed the jawbone of the Titanosaur, which

pointed in the direction of the stairwell we had used on Friday to get up to the area of the lab.

I lifted the velvet rope and we both ducked beneath it.

Booker grabbed my wrist. "What happens if one of the girls wakes up?"

"Then she'll wake another one and that one will wake Katie."

"But we'll be gone," he said. "Won't they come after us?"

"Don't be ridiculous. Katie will think I've finally awakened to your coolness," I said. "She'll think we're off by ourselves. Hey, I let her be alone with Kyle at the rodeo. She'd never come looking for us."

I broke away from his grasp and powered on up the staircase, shining my small light on the steps.

"You don't think there'll be guards up here?" he asked.

"I asked Keisha, and she said the guards all stay around the entrances on the ground floor at night," I said. "So we should be okay."

At the top of the steps, inside the turret, the moon lit up the interior space. We knew the way back to the lab because of yesterday's scouting trip.

"You think it was fair to leave Katie out of this?" Booker asked as I started down the hallway, losing the moonlight behind me.

"Best friend I could ask for, Booker, next to you," I said. "But she gets skittish sometimes, so I need an experienced pro like you at my side."

"Because we're going to do exactly what, Dev, now that Keisha told us that you're not going to get any DNA off these fossils?" he asked.

"We're going to do exactly what the situation calls for. Sam says a good detective really needs to be flexible," I said. "Able to roll with the punches."

The wide corridor was totally dark, fifty yards out from the windows in the turret. I turned my beam back on, and walked forward until I reached the door of the lab.

"Is it open?" Booker asked.

I held up my left hand with crossed fingers and turned the knob with my right.

"What's the point of locking up old rocks when nobody even has a clue where they are?" I asked, joking with Booker. "Maybe it should be locked, but they all know things are pretty secure up here all day."

The door swung open to reveal more black space. I took a deep breath and stepped inside.

When I flashed my light straight ahead, the first thing I saw was the long worktable, where Katie's clutch was sitting—still a work in progress.

He raised his beam, too, and walked to the other side of the table.

"What an amazing thing this is," he said. He was leaning in over the clutch and studying each one of the eggs. "Just like you told me, it looks like the surface of the moon."

"Yes, but if I could just get one of these eggs out of the Ditch, imagine what it could tell us."

"What do you mean, Dev?"

"You heard Keisha," I said. "If we could just get to see what's inside one of these prehistoric things, we could find out whether it's feathered or not. I mean, Katie and you and I could write a paper before the Montana team does."

"Then it would still be Katie's big discovery, right?" Booker said.

"You bet. What a gift to her that would be."

Booker tapped lightly on the top of one of the eggs.

"It's a rock. You're the one who told us that. You don't have to be so gentle with it."

He laughed and knocked on it again like it was a closed door. Nothing budged.

"You don't really think you can get inside by pounding on it, do you?" I asked.

"Afraid not."

"And we can't move the clutch," I said, thinking out loud.

That's when I spotted a box of vinyl gloves on the end of the worktable.

"There you go, Booker." I was trying to get in the mind-set of a real detective. "We should put on gloves if we're touching things in here."

I pulled some out and we both put them on. I couldn't help but smile at the thought of my mentor, Sam Cody, working a crime scene in pajamas. Then again, a good cop went after trouble, wherever it was.

I turned my back to the table and faced the tower of shelves opposite it, which stretched from the floor of the room to its tall ceiling.

There were fossils of all shapes and sizes, stacked on top of each other, labeled by species and date. Some had locations of their finds written with bold marker, while others bore the names of individuals, whether scientists or dig volunteers there was no way to tell.

"The teeth and things from Montana must be closest in reach," I said. "Wouldn't you think?"

"I guess so," Booker said, examining the assortment of tools that were laid out on the worktable.

I was about to reach for a large fossilized bone on

the shelf in front of me when I froze in place, nailed there by fear.

"Did you hear that?" I whispered, standing dead still and turning off my light.

"Nothing," Booker said, shutting his off then, too. He waited a full minute before he asked, "What did your Atwells get?"

"Listen," I said. "Can't you hear it?"

Booker turned his head toward the door. "Barely, Dev. It's a really faint noise," he said, looking as scared as I was. "Is it footsteps?"

"Sort of. But too many of them to be so light."

The sound was confusing me. More than two feet moving in our direction, or so it seemed.

What if a guard had been summoned because someone had seen or heard us?

Suddenly, I heard a loud *bang*, like something crashing close by—maybe even in the room next to us.

I scooted around the table on my tiptoes, standing close behind Booker.

"Don't back down now," he said.

I straightened up and stepped beside him. If there was no other place to hide, I'd have to take the consequences for my actions.

I turned on my flashlight again, so as not to provoke any response from whoever was coming to find us.

The small beam prompted a reaction from whoever was stirring in the corridor.

"Have you got my back?" I asked Booker, speaking softly into his ear.

"Always, Dev."

I tiptoed closer to the heavy door and leaned against it, poking my head into the hallway.

I put one foot out and the culprits flew up at me, practically in my face, fluttering their wings and circling overhead in the hallway.

"Pigeons!" I said to Booker, running to the next lab adjacent to ours to check the source of the noise.

A large casement window had been left open—banging in the wind that must have come up since we arrived at the museum—and six or seven pigeons had flown in to seek shelter from the rain.

"Trespassers again, Dev," Booker said, breathing a sigh of relief. "Your dig seems to be haunted by trespassers."

25

"Ready to go downstairs, Dev?" Booker asked.

"Give me five more minutes in the lab," I said. "Steve wanted feathers on his dino. Why not just give him pigeon feathers with your bones and call it a night?"

I was padding back down the hallway to the lab while the birds were flitting around overhead, looking for ledges on which to perch.

"Because Keisha gave me an idea, Booker."

"Like what?"

"You check the shelves on the other side of the lab," I said, shining my light back on the spot where I was when I had been interrupted.

"What am I looking for?"

"Teeth and bones," I said. "Marked with Big Timber or Steve's name, or maybe Ling's. I want to find Katie's bones."

I ran my flashlight back and forth across the rows of specimens, but none of the ones within reach were more recent than a year ago.

"Ling Soo!" Booker called out, a couple of minutes later. "Looks like a couple of big teeth right here, the writing on the bag says, wrapped up with her name on them."

"Way to go, Booker," I said, dashing around the end of the worktable to join him in the hunt. "Now if we can just find something that says Katie Cion."

Booker reached his long arm into the space between shelves, behind the items labeled with Ling's name, and came out with some small paper bags.

"Any of these sound familiar?" he asked, reading them aloud. "They're all marked with the words Big Timber."

"Yes, I recognize some of them. They're the other grad students who were digging with Ling and Katie and me."

Booker put the bags back in place and came out with four more. He put two to the side. "Dev, I think I've got them."

"Them?"

"Two bags," he said.

"Katie found three bones our first afternoon," I said, holding out my gloved hand. "I thought they'd be all together in one single bag."

"Help yourself," Booker said.

I opened the bag and unwrapped the fossils, which were still packed in camel matting. There were three separate bones, just as I remembered.

Booker opened the second bag. "Three bones in here, too."

"Maybe Katie was right after all," I said. "Maybe Chip or Steve swapped out her bones for different ones. Let's compare them."

Sure enough, one set of fossils was larger than the other.

I picked up the two bags. The ones with the smaller bones was marked Return to KATIE CION with the date of her find. The writing on the second bag said KATIE CION***, with three asterisks—maybe one for each fossil, is what I was thinking—and the same date.

I leaned in over the bones—smaller ones first and then the larger ones—holding my light directly above them, turning them from side to side.

"Don't you have any photos of them from the dig site?" Booker asked.

"We didn't think fast enough," I said. "We never expected that they'd be taken away from Katie right there on the spot."

"Well, did you bring your phone up here with you?" Booker said, putting his hand out for it.

"Nope."

"Want me to go downstairs and get it?"

"Nope," I said, rewrapping the six bones and putting them in the same bags that Booker had found.

"You should take photos, if you're so suspicious, Dev."

"Here's the deal, Booker," I said, swiveling to face him. "I've figured out what to do. It's all become clear to me in these last few minutes."

"What's that?" he asked.

I handed him the bag with the smaller bones—the ones either Steve or Chip had substituted for the ones Katie actually found. "Would you mind reaching in and putting those back where you found them?"

"Sure," Booker said, replacing the first bag. "How about the one you're holding?"

I didn't answer him directly. I had just this single opportunity to convince him my plan was the right thing to do.

"Do you remember the time in second grade when I fractured my wrist?" I asked. "I had that bad fall when we went skiing with your parents, but I didn't complain about the pain till we got back to the city from upstate?"

"Yeah, Dev. Your arms and legs were all over the place that afternoon on the slopes."

"And where did your mother take me when we got back to the city?"

"I'm not sure I remember. Did we go to a hospital?"

"No, she took me first to her office, so she could do a scan of my wrist."

"A CT scan," Booker said, like the idea was slowly dawning on him. "Computerized tomography scan."

"Yeah. At the time," I said, laughing at the memory of the much-younger me, "I thought your mom was talking about an X-ray machine that was used on cats. A CAT scan. I didn't know tomography meant waves that can penetrate to see inside things."

"Oh, no you don't, Dev," Booker said, reaching out for the bag I was holding, just as I moved to put it behind my back.

"Keisha said it herself, Booker. We need to see what's *inside* these very bones that made Steve or Chip or Ling want to keep them for themselves."

"This is the point where your mother says it with your full name," Booker said, shaking his head. "It's not happening, Devlin Quick."

"A CT scan is all," I said. I didn't get what Booker's objection to that idea could possibly be. "I know your mom will do that for me. Plus there's nothing to break or damage with these little old guys—they're just ancient pieces of rock."

"But, Dev," Booker said, sounding as though his voice had deepened by an octave as he pleaded with me, "you can't take that bag out of here."

I was already on my way through the door.

"You can't steal those bones," he said, raising his voice even louder.

"For your information," I said, turning to face him. "I'm not stealing anything. I would never condone a theft."

I paused, to make him understand my purpose.

"I'm borrowing the bones," I said.

"But you can't do that! They belong to—to, uh, to Steve or to—whoever paid for the dig."

"Let me explain the law to you," I said, holding the bag up at eye level and swinging it back and forth. "The law of the land in Montana."

"But—"

"It's Katie who found these fossils," I said. "And she dug them up on private property, not on public lands. Her dad called the rancher who owned the dig site and got his permission to let Katie keep them."

"He did?" Booker asked.

"Yup. Just this week," I said.

"How come he didn't want to claim them for himself?"

"Because he told Katie's dad that he doesn't have any kids, and he was happy that she was so interested in such important scientific work," I said. "Beside that, he's got so much land he probably thinks he has a shot at finding more bones."

"Cool," Booker said.

"So the law is quite clear that this little fragment of some duckbill dino is entirely owned by my best friend, Katie Cion. I promise I'll return them to the museum in a couple of days, but for now I'm borrowing these bones."

26

"Wake up," Katie said, shaking my shoulders. "I'm really hungry."

I must have been the last one in the group to open my eyes.

"I am, too," I said. "Where is everybody?"

"The girls are in the bathroom getting dressed. Booker, too," Katie said. "So we can go back to the food court for breakfast before the museum opens."

I got off the cot, rolled up my sleeping bag with the small bones still tucked inside it where I had put them before I went to sleep, and took my clean clothes down to the bathroom to catch up with the others.

I have to make the point that carrying the truth around—whether inside your head or wrapped in a piece of camel matting—is an awfully large burden for a kid to bear. But I had undertaken this investigation with a plan to see it through to the end.

I thought about telling Katie what Booker and I had done, but I really wanted her to enjoy her birthday with a clear conscience.

Natasha and our friends were all laughing and talking as we ate, but I was sort of anxious to be on our way.

We all left the museum in late morning, and once I got home I pretty much had the day to myself. When I went into my bedroom, I hid the bag with three bones under my pillow.

Then I went for a bike ride along the promenade by the East River, and took Asta to the dog run in Carl Schurz Park.

I had dinner at Lulu's house, which was always a pretty special occasion. She has a cook named Bridey, who loved to spoil me by making my favorite dishes, even though Lulu would have preferred that I ate a proper meal along with her.

Once I told Lulu about some of the adventures of the Montana dig, she came pretty close to cracking me. She kind of figured out that something had been going on with Katie's bones, and tried to get me to spill the beans about things while I was enjoying my grilled cheese and bacon sandwich.

Lulu had a great sense of adventure. She knew I was up to something, but she was cool with the fact that I wasn't telling any secrets about Katie quite yet.

"You know you can always confide in me, Devlin," she said, holding me by my shoulders and kissing me on both cheeks as I got ready to leave. "Everyone on earth needs one person like that, you know?"

"I do know that, Lulu," I said, smiling back at her. "I've always known that about you."

"You seem rather distracted tonight, dear," Lulu said, without letting go of my shoulders. "Your mother told me you've been spending a lot of time at the Museum of Natural History these last few days. Perhaps you need some more sunshine instead."

"I'm kind of fascinated by the things I'm learning about fossils, Lu."

"Bully," she said.

I figured she meant someone was forcing me to be inside the dark corridors with all the old fossils.

"No, no, Lu. No bullies at all," I said. "I really like it there."

"Bully, my dear, was Theodore Roosevelt's favorite phrase. It means 'grand,' Devlin, or 'most excellent,'" she said.

"I didn't know that." I was trying to get on my way—a short walk to home.

"You're right in his mold, young lady. He didn't like 'mollycoddlers' a bit, if I remember my history," Lu said. "He didn't like people who were morally soft."

"Soft?" I asked.

"You act, Devlin," Lulu said. "You act when you encounter a wrong. And there's nothing more important than to do that. Your father was that way—and your mother is, too. It's in your genes, dear, and I like that about you."

I turned to get onto the elevator, then looked back at Lulu. "You don't happen to have any paleontologists in your address book, do you? You know everyone, Lu."

"Bone diggers?" she said, taking a few moments to think. "I'm afraid that I don't."

"Thanks anyway, Lu. See you next weekend," I said, blowing her a kiss as the doors closed.

Hours spent with my grandmother always inspired me. Of course I would take action. I had proof that the bone diggers had messed with Katie's fossils.

27

"Where's your mom working today?" I asked Booker when we met up at a West Side coffee shop on Monday morning.

"No surgery scheduled," he said. "She's in her office."

"Which one?" Aunt Janice had two of them, one on Martin Luther King Boulevard in Harlem, near the home in which she'd grown up, and another closer to Roosevelt Hospital on Fifty-Ninth Street.

"Monday and Friday she's in Harlem," Booker said.

"That's good," I said. "Anyway, we're closer to Fifty-Ninth Street."

Booker finished his iced tea and looked up at me as I motioned him to get going. "You sure you want to do this?"

"Actually, I had dinner with my grandmother last night, and she's one hundred percent behind me."

"She knows all about it?"

"Enough, Booker. Lulu knows quite enough," I said.

"Are you a man of action, or not? A mollycoddler or—?"

"A what?" he said, pushing back his chair and throwing his plastic cup in the trash.

"It's a Teddy Roosevelt thing," I said.

I had worn a cross-body bag with a thick strap, so that the pouch with the bag of bones hung at my waist, in front of me where I could see it. I found myself patting it from time to time to make sure the package was safe.

We took the subway down to Fifty-Ninth Street and walked a few blocks west till we got to the building where Janice Dibble had her office.

Booker opened the door and we went inside.

"This brightens my day," Tina, the receptionist, said. "It's nice to see you both, but I assume you know that your mother's at—"

"Yeah," Booker said, "in the Harlem office."

"Actually, she's in surgery right now. There was a bus accident in midtown and she's got a whole lot of fractures to take care of."

"Will everyone be all right?" I asked.

"Now don't get all squeamish on me, Dev," Tina said. "Nothing Dr. Dibble can't fix."

Squeamish wasn't my problem today. Aunt Janice's ability to shut me down was the bigger issue.

"Is Harry here?" Booker asked.

Harry was Aunt Janice's tech guy and had worked with her for years.

"He sure is," Tina said. "He's got a couple of procedures booked for later today. Want to see him? Just go on in the back."

"Yes, ma'am," he said.

"Hey, Harry," Booker said, once we got into the examining area and found him at his computer, entering data on medical records.

"Booker!"

They high-fived and we hugged, then caught up on things.

"What brings you here?" Harry asked.

"You tell him, Dev," Booker said, less than enthusiastically.

I explained that Katie and I had been on a dig. Harry knew who Katie was, from hearing Dr. Dibble talk about all of us, but he had never met her. I left out the mysterious elements of the story and asked him if he would be so kind as to do a CT scan of the three bones.

Harry didn't look any happier than Booker did. "Where are they?"

I unzipped the pouch and unwrapped them. "The

people who run the dig told us they're foot bones. Parts of the baby dino's feet, that is."

Harry smiled. "Small guys, aren't they? This will be easier than I thought. I was expecting something much larger."

"You know looks can be deceiving," I said. I was snapping photographs of the bones, which I wish Katie and I had done back at the dig site. "These could actually be from a super-duck. Super-duckbill, I mean."

"Started out little, like all the rest of us."

"I know that CT scans are expensive, Harry. And my grandmother will certainly pay for this, if you give me a bill."

I knew Lulu would be only too happy to do that, in the name of science.

"Now, if I was doing this on Booker's brain, Dev," Harry said, "he's got so much info jam-packed in there that it might cost you thousands of dollars."

"Really?" I said.

If there had been an emoji of my face to capture the moment that Harry put a price tag on the scan, it would have been a frowning expression. Maybe it even would have been an emoji with a single tear rolling down her cheek.

"I had no idea. I mean, I know it's a full house up

there in Booker's head, but I didn't know how expensive the scans are. Aunt Janice didn't charge us anything when I had mine done."

"You're family, Dev. This critter with fossilized bones didn't go to Vassar College with your moms," Harry said. "Not to worry. This will just be a couple of hundred dollars."

I gulped. "Okay," I said, trying to think how old I would be if I took some money out of my allowance every week to pay Lulu back. Probably eighteen. Maybe twenty. I'd be in college then and hopefully still getting an allowance or having a job to get me through.

"What are you looking for, exactly?" Harry asked, making a soft bed for the fossils on the cushion of his machine.

"Um—I'm not exactly sure," I said. "What do you think I should be looking for?"

"Beats me, Dev," Harry said.

"Well, one of the museum people told us the most important thing about ancient bones is what's inside them. Things we can't see by holding them or touching them."

"I believe that. CT scans will show you things that even X-rays can't do."

"Why is that?" I asked.

"That technology was invented more than one hundred years ago."

"Wilhelm Röntgen," Booker said. "A German professor."

"S.O.S!" I spurted out, rolling my eyes. Lulu was right, though. If I rolled them too often, the move lost all its effect.

"What's that supposed to mean, Dev?" Booker asked.

"Show-Off in Science," I said. "You do it all the time."

"There's stuff I know more about than you," he said. "You don't have to make everything a competition, you know."

"So Röntgen's discovery was a scientific bombshell," Harry said, adjusting the settings on his machine. "Docs could see inside the body without performing surgery on the patient. The X-rays created images like individual slices through the human body. Painlessly."

"But they couldn't see through bones, could they?" Booker asked.

"That's right. Just soft tissue. But that's what makes CT scans so amazing, because they can cut through human bones, too," Harry said. "I've just set the radiation dose to a much higher level. Then we'll step out of the room and see what's inside these fossils, okay?"

"Why is the dose higher?" I asked.

"The human body couldn't withstand what these little old fossils can, Dev. My machine is making thousands of radiographs through the rock, rotating a degree or so between images."

"What will the results tell us?" I asked. I was getting really excited now.

"Well, the software puts all the images together and kind of reconstructs your fossils, knitting the sliced images together into a 3-D graphic for you, if we get lucky," Harry said.

"What would be *un*-lucky?" I asked as Harry closed the door behind us, and I pressed my nose against the glass window, watching as the cushioned platform was guided into the cylindrical scanner—a giant steel doughnut with Katie's three fossils disappearing into the center hole.

"Your bones could be too dense," he said, "or crystallized, which wouldn't give us a very clear picture of what's inside there. Or maybe this machine just won't be as powerful as a special CT for paleontological work."

"Fingers crossed, then, Booker," I said, turning to him and holding both hands in the air. We were hoping for clues that the fossils were actually from the same animal and that they actually belonged together. "Fingers and toes, okay?"

Harry worked the controls as I fidgeted behind him. Booker was sitting in a chair at Harry's desk, playing a game on his phone.

"What's taking so long?" I asked, after fifteen minutes had passed.

"I'm shooting photographs, Dev. X-rays," Harry said. "CT scans are sophisticated X-rays—think of them that way. Thousands of them. Are you always this impatient?"

"I think that's a result of her name," Booker said, without looking up from the screen. "When she races at a swim meet, her team cheers her on by shouting '*Quick*-er, *Quick*-er.'"

"Well, another five minutes and I'll be done, Dev."

I sent a text to Liza. "*¡Hola, mi amiga!* Did your mom find out anything about Steve Paulson?"

I doubted she'd answer right away, so I e-mailed several other friends until I heard Harry turn off his machine.

"Done?"

"As much as I can do, Dev."

He opened the door to the scanning room and pressed the button that slowly ejected the bed on which the fossils were resting.

"Okay if I wrap them up?" I asked.

"All yours."

I carefully replaced the three bones in their safe packaging while Harry went back to his office. When I rejoined him, he had taken Booker's place at the desk.

"What did you learn, Harry?" I asked.

He was printing out the results of the scan. Somehow, all the jumbled slices and slivers of the fossils were coming into focus as super-sophisticated X-ray images of Katie's discovery.

"You know how it goes, Dev," Harry said, leaning in to study the photograph. "The tech can't give the patient a diagnosis. We have to wait for the doctor."

"But, Harry," Booker said, "we need an answer now."

"Besides, I'm not the patient," I said. "The dino's been dead for millions of years and Aunt Janice was never his doc."

"Okay, okay!" Harry said, holding both arms up in the air. "I just don't want to get in the middle of a battle here."

"Booker and I aren't fighting over this," I said.

"Well, someone's not being straight with you," Harry said.

"What do you mean?" I asked, leaning in to look over his shoulder at the image he'd produced. "What are you talking about?"

I didn't know the first thing about reading a scan. The bones looked just like they had the first time I saw them out in Big Timber, only now with that X-ray look of a Halloween costume.

"You and Katie were told these were foot bones?" Harry asked.

"Yes. See that shape on the end?" I asked. "Everyone told us that was sort of a socket that connected these pieces to the next part of the dinosaur's leg."

Harry groaned and moved his head from side to side.

Booker put down his phone and crowded in next to me. "What's going on?"

Harry split his computer screen and brought up another scanned image to the right of the one we were looking at. "So this is a scan of a part of the body of a human being, from a reference book I use."

I looked from left to right. The shapes of all the objects—Katie's fossils and this sample scan—were pretty much the same. "What's your point?"

He picked up a pencil and pointed the tip of it at one of the dino fossils. "That socket you're talking about doesn't look like part of a super-duck foot at all. Whoever told Katie this was a foot bone was either badly mistaken—maybe an amateur in the field—"

"Katie and Kyle and I were the only amateurs at the

dig," I said. "Everyone else was pretty savvy on dinosaurs."

"Then maybe," he said, turning his head to look me in the eye, "maybe someone was lying to Katie."

"What about?" I asked.

"Why would anyone lie about a dinosaur fossil?" Booker asked. "I've got to hand it to you, Dev. You've been suspicious about the way Katie's bones were handled from the beginning."

"Too early for kudos," I said to Booker, staring at the screen, feeling a sudden chill. I heard Harry say the word "lying" and goose bumps ran up and down my arms. "We've got so much to figure out here."

"So if these aren't foot bones, what are they?"

Harry moved the pencil to the right, to the scan of human bones. He started to describe the lines and cracks and marks revealed on the interior of the fossils by his scan. "I'm willing to bet you have pieces of the tailbone here, Dev. Parts of a dinosaur's tailbone."

"Tailbone, foot, femur—what difference would it make?" I said, turning away from the scan. "We owe you for doing this, Harry, but I guess now we need a paleontologist."

I thought about it, then snapped my fingers and

turned back to the screen. My goose bumps were growing by the second.

"Because the tailbone is way more valuable than a piece of the dinosaur's foot," I said.

"Why's that?" Booker said.

"It's like teeth," I said. "Teeth and tailbones can help you identify a species. A little fossil in the foot isn't enough to prove something like that."

"Is Dev right, Harry?" Booker asked.

"In humans," Harry said, "that's the last vestige of where a tail used to be, right at the bottom of the spine. So look how similar the shape of our tailbones are to the ones Katie found. Could be Dev's got a point."

"I'm telling you, Booker," I said, picking up my package and placing it in my cross-body bag, "I smell a rat in the middle of all these lizards."

"But why would those bone diggers in Big Timber want to hide a fossil that could identify a new kind of dino?" he said.

My brain was in motion and all my wheels were spinning.

"I'm working on an answer for us," I said. "I really am. The only thing I know about those guys is that I think they'd lie to us faster than you can say Titanosaur."

28

"Now what?" Booker asked, on our way out of his mother's office. "You've got to get Katie's fossils back into the museum before anyone figures out they're missing."

"Understood," I said, checking my e-mails for word from Liza. "This might be the time to confront Steve anyway, now that I've got a copy of our CT scan."

"You're going to admit to him that you stole—I mean borrowed—the bones?"

"I don't see any need to do that."

"Then how do you plan to—?"

"First we call upstairs," I said as we started to walk north in the direction of the museum, "and I ask Steve if he'll talk to me."

"He didn't seem any too happy to see you on Friday, Dev."

"Now I've got evidence, Booker. The tide has turned." That was one of Sam's favorite expressions. If it worked for him in his developing investigations, I'd make it work for me.

"What evidence? If you tell him about the CT scan, he'll know you took the bones, and then he could make real trouble for you—for us—with your mother."

"Didn't you see me taking photographs of Katie's fossils before Harry scanned them?" I asked. "Steve won't have any way of knowing if I took those when we found them out west, or today."

"So you think he'll talk to you?"

"Yup," I said. "And while he does—while I keep him busy—you'll slip the bones back on the shelf where you found them."

"Seems risky to me, Dev."

"We'll be together," I said. "Totally together in the same room. Do you really think what detectives do every day doesn't have risks? We'll just be talking to a paleontologist in a laboratory inside the world's most famous museum, surrounded on all sides by security guards."

"I'd feel a whole lot better if Liza's mom had come up with some information about your guy."

"I'll tell you what," I said. "Why don't you shoot Liza a text right now? She'll get back to you pronto, I'm sure. She's so into you."

"Stop joking around, Dev."

We stopped at the next light and Booker sent off his

greeting to Liza with our question, pressing her for an answer.

We crossed the street and I could feel my phone vibrating in my pocket.

"Mom?" I said, seeing her number pop up as I went to answer the phone. "Is everything okay?"

"Yes," she said. "Where are you?"

"Right now? I'm on the West Side, hanging out with Booker."

"That's good. What are you two going to do?"

"So funny you should ask that, Mom," I said. "We're just in the middle of making some plans right now. We haven't quite figured it out yet."

Booker smiled and gave me two thumbs-up.

"Don't get caught in the thunderstorm this afternoon," my mother said. "At least that's what they're predicting. I'll treat you both to a movie at the multiplex on Broadway if you can't hit tennis balls with him."

"Thanks, Mom. Good idea." I didn't think Booker and I would need shelter from the storm if we were fortunate enough to get into the paleontology lab, but it was always good to have a backup plan.

"I just wanted you to know that Sheriff Brackley returned my call," she said.

"He did?" I said, jumping up and down in place. "Is it about Chip Donner?"

"It is, young lady."

"Let me put my cell on speakerphone so Booker can hear, too."

"I want you both to hear me," my mother said. "Loud and clear."

I didn't know if the frosty tone of her voice was Chip Donner's misfortune or mine.

"Go ahead," I said. "Did he steal a tractor?"

"What have I told you over and over again about keeping an open mind, Dev?" my mother said. "Chip was charged with taking a drift boat."

"A drift what?" I asked. "What kind of tractor is that?"

"I didn't say anything about a tractor. It's a boat," she went on. "It's the kind of boat fly-fishermen use on the rivers in Montana."

One thing I knew was that there were no boats on a dinosaur dig.

"But Tapp told me the guy was charged with stealing a motor vehicle," I said.

"It would seem that motor vehicles have a broader definition in Big Sky Country than in New York," my mother said. “Drift boats gliding down the rivers of Montana don’t even have motors. And furthermore, Dev, the sheriff told me that the charges will be dismissed on the next court date.”

“Bummer!” I said. “Why’s that? Because a drift boat isn’t a motor vehicle?”

“Because Mr. Donner apparently did not steal the boat,” my mother said. “He’s not guilty of any crime. It seems some kids took the vehicle out on the river for a joyride and abandoned it on the Donner property.”

“So I guess we’re still looking for an Atlas Road Warrior in Big Timber,” Booker said, “and someone who used it to trespass on the site.”

“That, and you shouldn’t have jumped to any conclusions about Mr. Donner, kids. Now get on your way and skip the street vendors with hot dogs for a change today. Get some yogurt and fruit, or something healthy for you.”

“Love you, Mom,” I said, kissing my phone so she could hear the sound of my smack. “Thanks for tracking that down for me.”

Booker and I continued to trudge our way toward the museum.

“So you think that eliminates Chip as a suspect?” he asked.

"I know I'm supposed to give him the benefit of the doubt, but it was actually Chip Donner who swapped out Katie's bones," I said. "He just grabbed them away from her."

"Then we'll have to talk to him, too," Booker said. "You've got to be thorough in this game. No stone left unturned."

We stopped in front of the museum to check our e-mails before going inside. "Look at this, Dev," Booker said.

He seemed excited as he passed his phone to me. He had received a reply text from Liza de Lucena.

I opened it and skimmed the personal part—how happy she was to hear from him and all that—and went right to the heart of it.

"My mom's made some calls to people she knows at the museum in Patagonia," Liza wrote, "but no one has ever heard of your Steve Paulson. We've both searched online for articles about the great dig, but same thing—there's no mention of Mr. Paulson or any wrongdoing. It looks like terminated just has the general meaning that it does in Spanish. If he was actually working on the project about the Titanosaur, then the dig finally came to an end."

I bit my lip and handed Booker's phone back to him.

"Not what you wanted to hear?" he asked, looking down at it.

"I guess my mom is right. We have to go where the evidence takes us, and so far we've only got a bunch of dead ends. My hunches are usually better than this."

"How about lunch?" Booker asked as I started to climb the museum steps. "How about we take a break now?"

"We're on a search for the truth, Booker Dibble," I said. "And that's not a 23/7 kind of job."

29

"Hello again," Booker said, working his smile on Zora Berke, the security guard he had charmed on Friday.

"How are you?" she said, returning the warm greeting.

"Have you seen Mr. Paulson today?" he asked.

I was taking the cross-body bag from around my neck and putting it over Booker's head.

"Those new people working in the lab?" she asked. "I don't know them by name yet. But if you do, young man, and they're expecting you, you just go right on up."

"Thank you, ma'am."

Courtesy, as Lulu reminded me all the time, takes you a good long way in life.

I removed the catch that held one end of the velvet rope in place and reclosed it after Booker joined me on the staircase that led up to the fifth floor. I was beginning to feel quite at home in the museum.

We made our way—this time with much greater confidence—through the windowed turret and partway down the hall to the small lab room.

The door was closed, so I knocked.

"Come on in," a man said. I recognized Steve Paulson's voice.

"It's just me, Steve," I said, taking a deep breath and stepping into the long narrow room.

He looked up from the documents he was studying, his back to the worktable and to the shelves to our right, from which Booker had retrieved the bones.

"You're making a regular nuisance of yourself, Dev, aren't you?" he said.

"Sorry about that. I really don't mean to be a pain. I'm so interested in everything you taught Katie and me that I thought I could write a paper for school about her discovery."

I had no trouble keeping his attention focused on me. I had that surefire way of getting under people's skin, like my mother often said, and maybe he thought by staring me down he'd get rid of me.

"I thought Katie was going to do that for her science class."

Booker was slowly making his way down the row

of shelves on the opposite side of the worktable. He appeared to be giving the fossils a casual browse.

"I think you know I adore Katie, Steve," I said, "but the truth is, we have different science teachers, and well, I'm a little better than she is at creative writing and—"

"Somehow, that fact doesn't surprise me," Steve said. "The creative part, I mean."

"Thanks for the compliment, sir," I said, even though I knew that praising me was not his intention. In fact, it was pretty snarky of him. "I can tell a really fantastic story about the dig if I just had a few minutes more of your time."

"Why don't you wait until I publish my own paper on these findings, Dev?" Steve asked. "Then I'll give you all the help you need."

"When would that be, if you don't mind my asking?"

Out of the corner of my eye, I could see Booker's hand reaching into the bag and coming out with the little pouch containing the bones. I had to keep needling Steve Paulson so Booker had a clear shot at replacing them.

"Another couple of weeks before I finish writing the whole thing up," he said. "But you can follow the first story in tomorrow's *New York Times*."

"That's beyond awesome, Steve," I said, stepping closer to look at the papers in front of him. "Even though you're not done with your essay?"

"It's a photograph, actually. Just a teaser for news of our discovery."

Steve's instinct for bragging seemed to outweigh my ability to annoy him.

"This picture?" I asked, keeping him focused on me while Booker got the job done. I tried to eyeball it but Steve moved it away from me.

"Tuesday's *Science Times*," Booker said, walking around the end of the worktable to stand on the other side of Steve, as though taking that path had been what he'd planned to do all along. "That's my favorite section of the week. May I see your photo?"

Steve ignored me and picked up the piece of paper with the Xeroxed copy of the photograph to show it to Booker.

Booker held it up and studied it. "I guess I'd have to be a dinosaur expert to know what's so special about this," Booker said.

"Let me have a look," I said, removing my phone from my pocket with my right hand and reaching for the paper with my left.

"By expert, Dev, I think your buddy is referring to me," Steve said, taking the paper back.

"I know that. I just wanted to look at it. To see what's so special about it," I said.

This time I wasn't going to miss the chance to take a snapshot of Steve's exhibit. As he held the paper up, I lifted my phone and snapped one. There had to be some paleontologist in the museum who could interpret it for me.

"Don't be posting that on Instagram before the *Times* gets it up online at midnight," Steve said, laughing at me, and pointing a finger at my phone. "Don't you go scooping me, Ms. Quick."

"No chance, Steve. I'm more of a *Times Book Review* fan than a science kid. But what is it exactly?"

"You saw the press conference on Thursday night, didn't you?"

"We did," I said. "My mom and I saw it."

"This photograph is proof, Dev," Steve said, waving the paper in his hand. "It's proof that our team has identified a new species of dinosaur."

"Your team?" I asked. "Or Ling Soo?"

"Ling's part of my team," he said, losing his toothy grin.

"Then where are the feathers? Isn't this all about dinos with feathers?"

Steve turned the piece of paper facedown and placed it back on the table in front of him. "Check it out in the newspaper, Dev. You'll see the feathers. You'll see what makes this so special."

"If it's all about her discovery," I said, "then why isn't Ling here?"

Steve just glared at me, as a large shadow rose up and loomed over our heads. I could tell from the look on Booker's face that something was wrong.

My head swiveled around. Chip Donner was standing in the doorway. I hadn't heard him approach.

"Chip!" I sort of stammered his name a couple of times. "Good to see you. This—this is my friend, Booker Dibble."

"Howdy," Chip said, nodding his head at Booker, but also blocking my way out of the small lab room. "I heard you talking about Ling. She asked me to send you her regards, Dev."

"Is she here?"

"I told you on Friday that she's back at school," Steve said.

"Oh, okay," I said, taking a few steps toward the door. My knees were shaking a bit, but I didn't want to show the two guys how nervous I was. "C'mon, Booker, we've got to go."

Chip Donner stepped to the side.

Booker walked back around the table and past Chip

into the hallway. I was about to follow him, but turned back to Steve.

"By the way, Steve," I said. "I almost forgot the most important thing. I came by to pick up Katie's bones—you know, those fossils she found the first day we were on the dig."

Steve got up from the stool he'd been sitting on.

"I wish I could give them to you, Dev," he said, shaking his head, "but I can't release them to anyone except the rightful owner."

I hoped Steve and Chip didn't notice what deep breaths I was taking as I tried to face them down, at the same time that Booker was pulling on my shirttail.

"I'll just call her up then," I said. "Booker and I can wait for her to come over here, if you don't think I have her permission to take them."

"What I think," Steve said, taking a step in my direction, "is that you two don't even have permission to be up here in my laboratory. I'm sure security can help me escort you out. Chip, you want to call for a guard?"

"We're going," Booker said. "We'll save you the trouble."

"Besides, young lady, you don't know the first thing about those fossils Katie found."

"You'd be wrong about that, Steve," I said, holding my

phone up. "I've even got photographs of Katie's bones."

I wasn't so much meaning to shake the phone at him as much as I couldn't quite control the way my hand was trembling.

Steve Paulson glanced over at Chip. "You said no pictures—"

"She's bluffing you, Steve," Chip said, sneering at me while he answered Steve. "That Katie's a good kid. She handed her three bones right over to me. Dev didn't take any photographs. She didn't have time, even if she'd wanted to."

"That would be wrong, guys," I said.

They were as much as acknowledging that the ones they had given back for Katie to sleep with that night in Montana had been substitutes. Neither one of them bothered to make the point that I could have taken snapshots then.

"I've got them right on this phone," I said as Booker tugged at me harder.

Chip turned and reached for my arm, but I was faster than he was.

"It's all backed up on my computer anyway, Steve," I yelled as I ran after Booker toward the staircase. "If you stole something from my friend Katie Cion, you can be sure Booker and I will figure it out!"

30

I was totally out of breath. Booker and I had raced down five flights of stairs and out onto West Eighty-First Street.

"Keep running, Dev," he said. "They may have sent security after us."

"We didn't do anything wrong," I said.

"By your mother's standards, or just by yours?" Booker asked.

"In that case," I said, reaching out to high-five his hand, "let's jog on."

We kept trotting across the broad avenue and into the cooler green coverage of Central Park. Clouds were forming overhead and the humidity was twizzling up the ends of my hair.

"We need to find Ling," I said.

"She must be up to no good, Dev. It seems like she doesn't want to be found."

"Let's make that our office for the next hour," I said, pointing to a park bench in a shady spot. "All I know is that Steve sure doesn't want us to connect with her."

"Of course not, Dev. She's in league with them."

"Steve and Chip are too big for us to take on, but you're almost as smart as Ling and I'm as tall as she is. She may not be their weakest link, but I'd say we have no choice except trying to divide her from them—"

"And conquer," Booker said. "Divide and conquer, Dev. I like it."

"I'll make some calls," I said, "if you scout up some lunch."

"There's a deli on Columbus. I'll be right back. Yogurt and fruit good?"

I nodded. My mother would appreciate that I agreed with some of her ideas. Our lunch menu was no reason to create an issue.

I opened my phone and dialed information. "Yale University in New Haven, Connecticut, please."

When the robotic operator gave me the number, I pressed to call through. It took me four times to get to the Paleontology Department and into their library. I knew the administrative offices couldn't give me official information about whether Ling was enrolled, but surely there was someone who had developed a relationship with such a smart student in a small unit of the university.

"Hello?"

A human voice actually answered. I sat up straight and hoped my most mature voice would emerge.

"Hello, madam? Are you a librarian?"

"Yes. Yes, I am."

"Good afternoon. My name is Devlin Quick."

I wanted to tell her how much I love librarians, how my Ditchley librarian made my life better every day of the school year by introducing me to good books and characters who would be my lifelong friends. But I thought it might be overkill. I needed to stick to my mission.

"I'm a student of paleontology," I continued. Those were my temporary credentials, of course. "And I'm afraid I'm very confused at the moment."

"About what? Are you a student here?" she asked.

"No, no. I'm in New York. And it's not fossils I'm confused about, I'm just trying to find a colleague of mine who was a student at Yale," I said. "I was on a dig with her just recently."

"All right, then."

"It's just that I can't find her, and I know your department has its own library, and I'm hoping you can tell me if she's been around lately."

"I'm not an information system, Ms. Quick. What school do you attend?"

"Her name is Ling Soo," I said, ignoring the question she asked. "I'm looking for Ling Soo."

The librarian didn't speak for several seconds.

"I'm afraid I can't help you, Ms. Quick. I was very fond of Ling," she said. "I thought she had a very bright future, but she isn't enrolled here any longer."

"What happened?" I asked. "Why not?"

"All I've been told is that she's returning home to China."

"So suddenly?"

"Yes," the librarian said. "Quite abruptly. If you'd like to leave your name and number, I'll be happy to pass it on if Ling gets in touch with me."

"Yes, please do," I said, spelling my name and leaving my cell number. "Thank you for the information."

So that piece of the puzzle was true. Ling Soo had withdrawn from her graduate program at Yale, even though she had made a breakthrough discovery in the Badlands of Montana.

"This doesn't make sense," I said to Booker, when he returned with our lunch. I devoured the cup of yogurt as though I hadn't eaten in days. "What if I reach out to her?"

"How come you didn't try that already?" Booker asked.

"I thought we'd run into her here at the museum," I said, "and I was worried that she might be part of what Steve and Chip were doing, so I didn't want to let them know we were onto them all."

"But you have her number?"

"I do," I said. "She gave it to Katie and me because she was supposed to be working here at the museum for a while after the dig."

"So, worst case scenario now is that she's back in China and you can't reach her," Booker said.

"Actually, the worst case scenario now," I said, "is that she gets in touch with Steve and says I'm trying to find her."

"He can't dislike you much more than he does right now."

"Good point. Should I call or text her?" I asked Booker.

"Text first."

I looked up her contact information and wrote a few lines. "Hey, Ling. It's Dev. Where R U? We need to talk." I threw in a few smiley faces to encourage her.

She must have been sitting on her phone.

"Whoa, Booker," I said as the balloon on my screen grew larger. "Ling's answering me."

"What about? Y?" she wrote.

"About the fossils you found."

"I can't," she texted back to me. "Going home to China tomorrow."

I gave up texting and dialed the number. "Ling? Ling, it's me. Please don't hang up."

She didn't say a word to me.

"The photograph of your big discovery is going to be online in the country's biggest newspaper at midnight."

"NO!"

"You didn't even know that the photo of the bones that confirm a new dino species is going public later?" I asked her. "Steve didn't tell you?"

"I am not talking to Steve," Ling said, in a voice so soft I could barely hear her.

"Why not?"

"Because I'm afraid of him."

"So am I, Ling! I'm afraid of him, too."

I could hear her sniffling. She didn't respond to me.

"Are you crying?" I asked. "You don't have to be afraid of anyone, Ling. My mother's the police commissioner of this city. She'll make you safe."

"Then why are you afraid, too?" she asked.

"Good question," I said. "I just saw Steve half an hour ago. He's been telling me to stay away from you since Friday, and now I'm getting scared. My mom can help both of us, I promise."

"Ask her where she is," Booker said.

"Where are you, Ling? Right now?"

Again, no answer.

"You can trust me," I said. "You'll have to trust someone."

"I'm staying at my friend's apartment, until I fly home tomorrow."

"Where is the apartment?"

"I can't tell you. I'm sorry. I'm afraid of everything right now."

"I'm with my best friend, Booker Dibble. He knows Katie, too," I said. "We don't have to come to you, if that's your safe place, but maybe you can meet us and tell us what's going on. We'll get you to my mom if that's what you need."

"Where are you two?" she asked.

"Just inside Central Park, across from the museum."

Ling was silent again for twenty seconds. Then she spoke softly. "I can't go to the museum."

"Understood."

"But my friend's apartment is very close by."

I tried to calm myself down so that Ling would be reassured.

"Booker and I can come to you, like I said."

Ling hesitated. "I'd rather come to you, if you don't

mind. The park is big, and there are a lot of people around."

My mind was speeding. We needed a private place to talk within a huge public park.

"I've got it. If you come in from the West Side near West Seventy-Ninth Street, there's a small cottage inside the park."

"A cottage?"

"Yes," I said. "It looks almost like a little schoolhouse. There are always lots of kids around it, because it's where puppet shows are put on."

"Kids. Okay. That sounds safe," Ling said.

Booker and I needed to get to the bottom of all this, as fast as we could. Ling didn't seem entirely ready to trust me at the moment, any more than I was sure that I trusted her.

31

"The Swedish Cottage?" Booker asked. "The Marionette Theatre? What made you think of that?"

"I remembered that your father took us there one day, back when we were really young," I said. "It's close to here, and it's just got a friendly feel to it, that's all. Not all those dead, stuffed things around you, like at the museum."

It only took us six minutes to wind our way south to the small building. The first time I went there, when I was about eight years old, I thought it really looked like a tiny house in Sweden. Apparently it was brought here for the 1876 Centennial Exhibition in Philadelphia.

"There's a show going on," Booker said as we approached it.

People were milling about on the grass surrounding the brown wooden cottage.

"Let's find out when it ends," I said, opening the door.

The long benches were filled with little kids—four- and five- and six-year-olds captivated by the marionettes—stringed puppets being worked by folks above the curtain, out of sight to the audience.

"Guess what?" I said to Booker. "The show is Pinocchio."

"That story is a good reminder for our talk with Ling," he said. "Pinocchio's nose grew longer every time he told a lie. We've got to get to the truth as fast as we can."

"I'll ask the questions and you can keep an eye on Ling's nose," I said.

"Deal."

I poked my head in and it didn't seem like there was long to go, so we hung out inside and watched until it was over. By the time the kids were applauding wildly at the finale, Ling was waiting for us outside the door of the cottage.

"Thanks for coming, Ling," I said. I felt kind of awkward, not knowing what each of us had to deal with. "This is my friend, Booker Dibble."

"Nice to meet you, Booker," she said. But she couldn't even force a smile.

Kids streamed past us, out of the tiny theater and onto the grass and walkway.

"There's a little room inside, next to the stage, where the three of us can sit and talk," I said.

Ling glanced around nervously, over her shoulder

and along the paved paths, and then followed us inside.

"Are you okay?" I asked.

She had been so confident when Katie and I first met her. But now she looked sad.

"In some ways, Dev, I don't feel the same. I'm not looking forward to going home."

"Are you leaving the United States because you're afraid of Steve?" I asked.

Her arms were crossed over her chest and she was leaning forward on her chair.

"I don't want to talk about him," Ling said.

"That's really strange," I said. "I thought we were going to talk about him. Isn't that basically why you came here?"

Ling paused before she spoke. "When we were in Montana, Katie told me about your sister. Your older sister."

"My sister? Oh, you mean Natasha. What did Katie tell you?"

"That she was originally from Moldova and that your mother helped her get asylum here, isn't that right?"

"Dev's mom can do most anything you need," Booker said.

"Do you know what a visa is?" Ling asked.

"I think so," I said. "It's kind of like a passport—a

document that lets you into our country, but only for a limited period of time."

Ling was rocking back and forth. "That's it. I was lucky enough to get a student visa so that I could go to graduate school at Yale. But now that I had to drop out of school, I'm going to have to go back to China."

"That's why you're leaving?" I asked.

"Yes, it won't be legal for me to stay in the United States. That is, unless your mother can help me get to the authorities who can issue me a new visa," Ling said. "There's no one else I would know to ask."

I needed to find out more about the situation before I could offer my mother's help.

"Natasha was the victim of a terrible crime," I said to Ling, who was staring at the floor. "That's how my mother met her. Has Steve—or Chip—has either one of them done anything to hurt you?"

I wanted to know why Ling wanted to stay here, but left Yale. I was hoping she'd give us a sign as obvious as the growth of Pinocchio's nose if I hit the right button. I really wanted to know if she was okay.

"No," Ling said. "No, no one has hurt me."

"Have they threatened to hurt you?"

"No," she said.

"Hmmm," I said, trying to think through this odd

situation. Had Ling really discovered fossils that announced an entire new species of dinosaur. "Did they steal something from you?"

"No, they didn't," she said.

"You know a theft would be a crime, right?" I said, staring at Ling's nose, which hadn't moved a fraction of an inch.

"But there is no theft, Dev." Ling looked at me for the first time since we had started talking.

"This photograph that Steve has—the one that he's making public tonight—did he take those fossils from you?" I asked. "Couldn't they belong to you, if you asked the ranch owner, since you found them on private land?"

"I can't make you understand this, I guess," Ling said, standing up and turning around, as though to leave. "You're not really paleontologists—you're just kids."

She really knew how to hurt a girl.

Booker answered before I could think of a snappy reply. "Try me, Ling. Try explaining what you want to tell us to me. You withdrew from Yale—but you don't want to go home—and you'd like a visa to stay here and go to school somewhere else?"

"You don't get it. All I want is Dev's mother to help me."

"Give us a little bit more," Booker said. "What do you think we don't understand?"

Ling stood her ground for a few moments, then opened up. "Steve Paulson's a bully. Tell me, is that a crime?"

Ling wasn't using the word "bully" the way Teddy Roosevelt meant it. I hated bullies—I hated them in the school yard or the swimming pool or the playground or on a hillside in Montana.

"I don't think every kind of bullying is a crime," I said, "but sometimes it is."

When my mother was a prosecutor, she had worked hard to make sure bullies who crossed the line could be punished. There were vicious cyberbullies who'd been arrested by the NYPD for online threats, and guys who harassed people in person, in subways and on the street. But sometimes it was just mean kids who were bullies—like a few girls at my school—and their bad behavior was beyond the power of the law.

"What exactly did Steve do to you?" Booker asked. He was standing tall, as ready to back up Ling as he always was to stand by me.

Ling was staring at the floor again.

"I'll call my mother," I said. "I promise."

"Your friend Katie," Ling said, in a voice barely above

a whisper, "she actually made the most important discovery of the dig."

"Her clutch of eggs?" I said. "The Ditch?"

"Yes."

"But Katie didn't find an entire new species," I said, stepping cautiously into a sensitive area. "You're the one who discovered that."

"Actually, I'm ashamed of what I did," Ling said.

"Ashamed? You should be so proud of yourself," I said. "This is no time to leave for home, Ling. You get to name the new species—the rare feathered duckbill dinosaur. We'll have to find a way to get you a visa."

Ling burst into tears.

"There's no need to cry," I said.

Booker reached into his jeans pocket for some napkins leftover from lunch and handed them to Ling so she could wipe her eyes.

"Do you remember those three bones that Katie found the very first afternoon?" I asked.

She squinted at me and answered with a question. "Why are you asking me that?"

"I think Steve and Chip thought they were important, too," I said.

I could see that Ling was frightened now. "I should never have agreed to meet with you," she said, heading for the door. "Your mother will never be able to get what I need."

"Steve switched the bones on Katie, didn't he?" I asked. "Or was it Chip who did that?"

I bolted ahead of Ling and stood in her way. "Those three little bones are at the heart of all this, aren't they?"

Ling didn't know which way to turn.

"Katie and Dev had that feeling all along," Booker said to Ling. "Don't hold it in. Maybe we can stop Steve before he goes public with his photograph tonight."

Ling started crying again—sobbing this time. "Those three bones Katie found gave Steve Paulson exactly what he needed."

"Needed for what?" I asked. "Please tell me."

"We didn't find a new species of dinosaur in Big Timber, Dev," Ling said, wrapping her arms around me as I tried to comfort her. "It's a hoax. Maybe the biggest dinosaur hoax in history!"

"A hoax!" I said, pushing Ling back so I could see the expression on her face. "What?"

"I got caught in the middle of this terrible trick—a fossil that's really a phony—that Steve is trying to pass off as the real deal," Ling said, looking from Booker's face to mine with a desperate plea. "I had to withdraw from Yale. I have to leave. I won't be safe here unless you and your mom can help me."

"I've never handled a hoax before," I said. "But we've got to stop Steve before he causes any more harm."

32

"Do you know where my mother is, Tapp?" I asked, pacing around the small room in the Swedish Cottage.

"That's one thing I always know, Dev."

"Can you put me through to her?"

"She's not picking up her phone. There's a hostage situation at a bank in the West Village. The commissioner's with the Hostage Squad now."

"How about Sam?" I asked.

"He's right in the middle of things, too," Sergeant Tapply said. "Since when won't I do?"

"You'll do fine. You just need to tell my mom to call me as soon as possible."

"Is everything all right, Dev?" Tapp asked.

"Under control at the moment, but Booker and I are going to need her help," I said, looking over at Ling, who had taken a seat on the side of the room. "And tell her my friend Ling needs some guidance for renewing her visa. Like tomorrow."

Ling picked her head up and smiled at me.

"You and Detective Dibble need backup, Dev?" Tapp asked. "Is it urgent?"

"We're good at the moment," I said. "We're in the Marionette Theatre inside Central Park."

"Don't get yourselves tied up in any puppet strings, young lady," Tapp said, chuckling at me, which probably wasn't his best response option. "What's the offense?"

"We've been hoaxed, Tapp. It's a pretty serious thing. Booker and I are working with the vic. If I need you to find me a crime, I'll get back to you with the facts."

"And I'll see the commissioner gets your message."

"Did you hear that, Ling?" I asked. "The man I was talking to is my professional lifeline to my mom. She's in the middle of a case right now, but she'll call as soon as she gets a break."

"Thank you both so much. I will be so grateful to meet her."

"Do you feel better now?" Booker asked.

Ling nodded her head.

"Where do you want to start, Ling? You need to tell Booker and me the story."

We had drawn three chairs together and waited till Ling looked comfortable and seemed secure enough to talk with us.

"I met Steve Paulson at a conference in Washington, DC, last winter," she said. "It was at the beginning of my second semester at Yale. It was only for about fifty or sixty scientists and was entitled 'Dinosaurs Among Us.' Also people like Steve, who don't have advanced degrees but have done a lot of work in the field, were invited to attend, too."

"How did you find each other, exactly?"

"I think it was the second day of the conference, after I delivered a paper in a small seminar room."

"You did? You gave a talk at a convention for paleontologists?" I asked. "That's really impressive."

"I was very honored to do it," Ling said.

"What was your topic?" Booker asked.

"It was basically about the dig I had trained on in the Gobi Desert. It was a description of what we did there, and a PowerPoint with all the pictures I had taken and the fossils that we found."

"You told Katie and me about your Gobi trip the night we met you," I said.

"Well, Steve was really excited to find someone who had actually participated and who could tell him more about the project," Ling said. "He flattered me so much that I should have thought twice about his interest, but then it's really only paleontologists who are into the Gobi stories."

"Count me in," Booker said. "Dev told me you were at the Flaming Cliffs."

"Yes, I was," she said. "It's an amazing place. So Steve took me to lunch and we traded stories—he told me about the dig for the Titanosaur in Patagonia and I talked about the Gobi."

"Was he curious about anything in particular?"

"At first," Ling said, "he was mostly interested in the state of paleontology in China."

"Why?" I asked. "Is something special going on there?"

"I wouldn't call it special," Ling said. "I'd call it a good place for your mother to send some of her detectives."

My ears perked up at that remark. "Detectives? For what kind of crime?"

"I think I need to explain how different things are in my country," Ling said. "Most of the time, in China, it's not scientists or students who dig up fossils."

"How come?"

"We have some provinces in the northeast which are badlands, too. Lakes and marshes, where there were once a lot of volcanic eruptions, which are so good for preserving the ancient bones," she said, calming now as she spoke. "But that part of our country is so poor that many of our farmers are the ones who are collecting the specimens."

"Are the farmers trained?" Booker asked.

"Not at all. But they know they can make a lot of money—tens of thousands of dollars—by turning over the dinosaur fossils to private dealers."

"That's called the black market, isn't it?" I asked. "What the farmer is doing is basically illegal."

"Completely so, but very hard to police in our remote provinces."

"That's crazy," I said. "No wonder you could use my mom's detectives."

"What's especially wrong is that when they make discoveries, the farmers destroy a lot of the scientific information that we need," Ling said. "If we can't document the location and the layers of rock from which the bones came, then we really can't be precise about their age, or how valid they are."

"I think I understand that," I said. "You guys were all so careful with every step of the dig."

"I get it, too," Booker said, pointing to a far corner of the room. "Like if I find a tooth over there, and then another bone in the next room, but I can't prove to you where I found them . . ."

Ling was nodding her head in agreement, this time with a smile. "You've got it, Booker. Then I can't really make a claim that they are from the same animal when I study them. The dinos from which they each came might have lived a million years apart in time, even though they were discovered on the very same farm in China."

"Whoa," I said. "That would make it really hard for you to prove things well enough to go to a museum, or a professional publication."

"Very hard to prove for those purposes."

"And that's what interested Steve?" I asked.

"I thought so at first," Ling said as the smile faded from her face. "But it was more sinister than that."

The lights in the small room flickered and I heard the roll of thunder way off in the distance.

Ling shuddered and looked up at the light fixtures.

"Don't worry," I said. "It's just weather. What did Steve want?"

"I didn't know at the time. In fact, I didn't know until he hired me for the dig and we reached Big Timber," Ling said. "But it was all about something that happened in China almost twenty years ago."

My mom always reminded me that when you're twelve, twenty years seems like an eternity. If you told me that woolly mammoths roamed the Earth twenty years ago, how was I supposed to know anything different? But I couldn't imagine how what Steve was interested in could affect Ling.

"So it was about a fossil that was stolen from China and sold on the black market?" I asked.

"No. That's what Steve wanted me to think he was interested in," Ling said as sheets of rain pounded against the windows of the cottage. "He had me totally convinced he was hiring me for the integrity of the scientific part of the dig."

"But that wasn't it?" I said.

"No, he was just using me. Like one of the puppets in the theater. All Steve wanted to do was pull my strings and control me."

"That's not your fault," Booker said, patting her on the knee. "Even Pinocchio was a good kid who got swept up in bad company."

"To do what?" I asked, stepping over to close the window so the rain didn't soak the cottage floor. "What did Steve want you to do, in particular?"

"He needed me to read all the scientific papers that

were published twenty years ago, in Chinese," Ling said. "After all, it's my first language."

"What were the articles about?"

"They were about one of the famous men who had pioneered discoveries in the Gobi Desert that teamed up with bone diggers from China to photograph and write about the find of a very rare feathered dinosaur in a province way out in our badlands," Ling said.

"A feathered dinosaur," I said, "just like your discovery in Montana."

Ling looked ready to cry again.

"Don't be upset," I said. "It was meant to be a compliment."

"What you need to understand, is that when the article about the Chinese flying dinosaur was published in your *National Geographic* magazine, twenty years ago," Ling said, "an American scientist was able to prove that the entire thing was a hoax. The amazing Chinese fossil had been faked, Dev."

"Faked? And they got as far as publishing an article about it in *National Geographic*?" I asked, thinking of the image that was about to go online in the *New York Times*. "They must have fooled an awful lot of smart people to get to that point."

Ling nodded her head. "Oh yes, they were very good at what they did."

"A faked fossil," Booker said. "But how did the bad guys do it?"

Ling was biting the nails on her right hand. "The Chinese paleontologists, who wanted to become famous around the world, used the legs of a tiny dinosaur—a juvenile, which was pretty rare in itself—and they attached those bones to the bones of another fossil, an entirely separate species—"

I couldn't stop myself from interrupting Ling.

"I bet the other body part of the fake was a tailbone," I said, thinking of Katie's find. It would be a natural part of the animal to attach to a fossil leg. It would explain why Katie's bones were stolen by Steve and Chip.

"That's it, Dev," she said.

"So the photograph that the Chinese released twenty years ago was just a cut-and-paste, not a real specimen?" I asked.

"It was artificially made from two different species, Dev," Ling said, looking up at me. "It was just a cut-and-paste—not the least bit real or rare—to try to fool the entire scientific community."

Booker snapped his fingers. "Just like Steve's about to do."

"But the tools we have for testing fossils now are so much better. Won't everyone know it's a fake?" I asked.

"Not before Steve makes his fortune and moves on to the next dig," Ling replied.

"We've got to stop him," I said, "before that photograph goes viral tonight."

"If Steve is faking these fossils," Booker said, "then the photograph he's giving to the newspapers is actually a forgery."

"Good thinking," I said.

"Forgery's a crime, Ling. It's right there in black-and-white in our Penal Law. I'm certain that the police commissioner will have something to say about this after all."

33

"Hey, Tapp?" I said, standing at the door of the cottage, looking out, hoping the rain would let up a bit. "Is my mom okay?"

"All clear at the bank," he said. "Everyone is safe and sound. If your mother hasn't called you yet it's just because she's briefing the mayor on how the hostage situation unfolded."

"Thanks so much. That's a relief," I said.

I worried about my mother's safety a lot. Sometimes I let it get in the way of my sleuthing. There was nobody in the world more important to me than my mom.

"The commissioner's a real pro, Dev."

"Oh, Tapp? If she gets to you before she calls me, will you please tell her that Booker and I are going over to the museum."

"Natural History?"

"Yep," I said. "We'll be in the dino lab trying to stop a first class hoaxer."

Tapp laughed. I hadn't meant to panic him, but I sure did want to be taken seriously.

"Get up to speed on your Penal Law, Sarge," I said. "Print out the section that defines forgery."

"I thought your specialty was theft, Detective Quick," Tapp said.

"You know how it is. You go where the evidence takes you."

"You want me to send some backup now?" Tapp asked.

"My mother and Sam will have us covered. Till then, it's just a bunch of us paleontologists having a tiff over creatures that died millions of years ago."

"Don't get in the way of any of 'em that breathe fire, Dev."

"Those would be dragons, Tapp, not dinos."

I hung up with Tapp and texted my mother. "Going to museum. Can U meet us there? Someone has been bullying our friend, and we think we've found him there."

I stashed the phone in my jeans pocket so I would feel it vibrate when she responded.

"Want to make a dash for it?" Booker asked. "We just have to run across Central Park West and up the steps of the museum."

"Give me a couple of minutes to put this together," I said.

"I think it's as together as it's going to get," Booker

said. "Those two guys, Steve and Chip, brought Ling into their project because she could translate all the documents from Chinese to English."

"Yeah, but—"

"It was an old hoax, and those men were going to try to work it all over again, with newer technology and better techniques. But in order to do that, Steve was smart enough to want to study the original hoax, in Chinese, to learn the details of what had gone wrong."

"So that photograph," I said, "is actually a forged instrument."

"Instrument?" Booker asked.

"That's what it's called in the Penal Law. My mom's handled lots of forgeries."

"So Ling is one of their victims," he said. "The first one, but not the last. Even President Sutton will have to buy into the results if nobody steps up to challenge them before this goes public."

I turned to look at Ling. "Both Steve and Chip are in this together?"

"I can't be sure of that," she said.

"Well, do you trust Chip?"

"I don't trust many people at the moment. I told you that," Ling said. "Mostly, he did whatever Steve asked him to do. I just assumed that they are partners in this."

"It's a good assumption," I said.

"There's one thing I need that will help me make my case to your immigration people, for my visa," Ling said.

"What's that?" I asked.

"I'm embarrassed to say it to you, because—well—Katie's your friend."

"You can tell Dev anything," Booker said. "She's a straight shooter. She doesn't hold a grudge."

"If I had those bones that Chip Donner took away from Katie, the first night of the dig, then maybe I can prove that I'm the one who doesn't want to go through with this illegal plan."

"They were tailbones, Ling, weren't they?" I asked. "That's what made them so special."

"That's right," she said. "Steve wouldn't have been able to carry out his plan until one of us found exactly the right fossil."

"And Katie Cion did," I said. "Because without a tailbone, the men could not have created the phony photograph that shows a new species. They absolutely needed a tailbone to work with. Even if they get caught later on, they might get away with faking it for now."

"I should never have let Chip take those pieces away from her," Ling said, putting her hands in her face. "I feel so badly about that. I knew what he was doing."

I stood behind her and rubbed her shoulders. "It's not your fault."

"But now we'll never be able to find them," she said. "We'll never get them back."

I looked up, over her head, at Booker.

"Just last week," she went on, "Chip told me they were in the care of a preparator, off-site of the museum. Chip said he couldn't get them back right away, that he couldn't put his hands on them for a while."

"Oh, I bet I can put *my* hands on them," Booker said, getting revved up for the task ahead.

"It's the perpetrators, not the preparators, who've got the bones," I said.

Ling looked up. "What do you mean?"

"The only thing standing between us and a colossal faked fossil scandal are a few raindrops," I said, taking my bag back from Booker and putting it around my neck and over my shoulder. "What do you say the three of us take on those bullies?"

34

Booker led the way out of the cottage and up the path to Central Park West. When the traffic light turned, he shouted to both Ling and me to run across the broad avenue and power up the steps of the museum.

We were all pretty well soaked by the time we got inside. The rain was coming down in sheets and the thunder sounded like it was getting closer and closer to us.

I stopped just past the security desk and took out my phone to check for messages.

"Anything from your mom?" Booker asked.

"Not yet," I said, speed-dialing another number.

"Then who are you calling?"

"Who do you think, Booker?" I said. "The rightful owner of the bones."

Katie answered the phone on the third ring. She whispered my name when she answered.

"Why are you talking so softly?" I asked.

"Can you believe I'm in my room? I'm not supposed to be using my phone because I'm grounded for the rest of the day."

"What for?"

"I said something stupid to my brother and he snitched on me."

"You can't be grounded today. Booker and I need you."

"We'll have to get together another afternoon," she said.

"This is not a social invitation or a date," I said as firmly as I could. "We're at the Museum of Natural History with Ling. And we're going to take possession of the first three fossils you found in Montana. You're the only one who can claim them, Katie. The only one."

"Maybe tomorrow."

"That will be way too late. Let me talk to your mom."

"She's not here. She's at the dentist right now. Too late for what?"

"I can't explain right now, but you've got to get yourself to the museum."

"My brother and his friends are between me and the front door. Do you expect me to just fly out the window?"

"Sorry! I don't mean to make it any worse for you,

that's for sure," I said. "And for what it's worth, whatever you said to your brother, he probably deserved it. I'll call you later."

I hung up and started walking down the long corridors with Booker and Ling, weaving our way through dioramas filled with mammals of all shapes and sizes.

We climbed staircases and finally got to the velvet rope that separated the floors of exhibits from the labs and storage rooms on the fifth floor.

"How did you ever find the lab room?" Ling asked. "It's not on any of the museum floor plans."

"Booker's great at making friends," I said.

I rehooked the rope behind us and we made our way up to the turret. The rain was beating so hard against the windows I couldn't see very far outside in any direction. There was a loud clap of thunder and then a streak of lightning that split through the fog like an arrow falling to the ground.

Ling was startled. Her hand flew to her chest.

"It's okay," I said. "We're inside, and it's just an electrical storm."

"Are you afraid of seeing Steve?" Booker asked.

Ling hesitated. "Not as long as you two are with me."

I took her hand and squeezed it hard. "Of course we will be."

I glanced at my phone as we approached the lab door, willing my mother to give me a sign that she was on her way here with Sam. "Booker, how many bars do you have on your phone?"

He looked at it. "No signal."

"That happens in lots of spots around the museum," Ling said. "These thick, heavy old walls make it hard to get reception."

"I vote we get started then," I said. "Why don't you knock on the door, Booker?"

"Ladies first, Dev."

I scowled at him, then made a fist and knocked.

"Enter." It was a man's voice, and it sounded muffled, probably because of the thick walls and oak panels of the door.

I motioned to Ling to stand off to the side, out of sight, and then I turned the handle.

"Well, well, well, Missy," Chip Donner said. "Seems like you just can't take 'no' for an answer."

"It's not a very good answer, Chip. Besides, Booker and I are looking for Steve."

"More nonsense about Katie Cion's bones, is it?"

"In fact, Katie should be here any minute now to claim them herself," I said.

"Good luck with that," he said, turning back to the newspaper he was reading.

It was a fiblet, but a small one, in the name of justice. I mean, she *should* have been there, the way I figured it. That part of wishing for it was true.

"Why don't you just scoot on out of here, Dev?"

"'Cause Booker and I are looking for Steve."

"Steve Paulson's the man of the hour, little lady," Chip said. "He's holding court down in the main conference room, giving all the bigwigs on the museum staff a preview of the *Archaeoraptor bigtimberus*."

The man didn't even have the courtesy to name the new species for Ling, after he'd used her in such a terrible way? I couldn't believe it.

"You heard me, Dev. This is no place for amateurs."

I took a deep breath and walked straight into the room to get right up alongside Chip Donner. I had to create a distraction to allow Booker to do his thing.

Booker followed my lead and walked around the other side of the table to the spot where he'd put Katie's bones.

"What's the part of 'get out of here' that you two don't understand?" Chip asked, looking around at Booker.

I tapped Chip on the shoulder, pulling up the photo

app on my phone, to get him to turn his attention back to me. "Want to see what I meant this morning, when I told you guys I had actually snapped a photograph?" I asked.

He did a double take as he grabbed the phone from my hand and stared at the picture.

"You didn't photograph this on a hillside in Montana," he said, raising his voice at me. "When did you get this shot?"

He was up from his stool and towering over me, making me back up toward the hallway.

"You'd better give that phone to me!" I said.

"Keep away from her, Mr. Donner," Booker shouted, coming between the tall Montanan and me.

I was through the door, nearly tripping over my own feet. I was scared of Chip, now that his temper was flaring and he had taken control of my only way of reaching my mom.

"I'm going to have to get security up here to move the two of you out," Chip said. "It's easier to get rid of vermin than of you and Booker."

"We're going to leave on our own," I said. "Just hand over my phone."

He was holding the phone way over his head in his

left arm. "Come pick it up tomorrow," he said. "From the museum's lost and found."

"My mom won't like that one bit," I said. "She's bound to come looking for it, Chip. She's certain to come right up here to your office."

"This time tomorrow, Dev, she can bring in her troops and look for us as long as she likes," Chip said, getting ready to slam the door in our faces. "We'll be on our way to the next dig."

"But my phone, Chip! You've got to—"

"Oops!"

Chip Donner slammed my phone against the floor and shattered its screen. I watched it skid across the room till it crashed up against the back workbench. "I hear the newer model is even better than this one," he said.

Then he kicked the door shut with his boot, banging it with a sound as loud as the thunder overhead.

35

"Follow me," Booker said, running in the opposite direction from the turret through which we'd come up to the fifth floor. Ling ran along with us.

When we reached the far end, we ducked around the corner and I tried to catch my breath.

"Better to come this way—no security guards right downstairs," he said.

"Did you snatch them back for us?" I asked. "Katie's bones?"

"You set up a good cover, Dev, even if it did cost you your phone," Booker said, removing the small pouch from his jeans pocket. "Here they are."

Ling's mouth dropped open. "You actually have the vertebrae that Katie picked up from the hillside? How did you find them?"

"That's a story for another time," I said. "It was a very Sherlockian deduction."

Booker handed the fossils to me and I tucked them carefully into my bag.

"What's in this for Steve and for Chip?" I asked Ling. "Besides fame."

"Make no mistake," she said, "if no one can call their bluff by doing a CT scan of the bones in that faked photograph, then Steve Paulson will be on the way to restoring his reputation and he can blame me for faking this. Someone might discover the hoax eventually, but not before tonight's announcement. And by then it might already be too late."

"Wait a minute," I said. "What about his reputation?"

"Then you don't know what happened in Patagonia, do you?" she asked. "About his work on the Titanosaur?"

"No!" I said. "I mean, we found a reference to the fact that Steve was terminated from that dig site, but not even my friend, Liza, who lives in Argentina, could find out why."

"The correct meaning of 'terminated' in this case would be 'fired,'" Ling said. "Steve was trying to poach some dinosaur bones in the same region as the dig."

"Are you kidding?" I said. "What happened?"

"The authorities caught him, but they agreed to drop the charges and not publicize the story in exchange for the return of the stolen fossils."

"Why would they do that?" Booker asked.

"I only heard the story recently," Ling said. "One of

my friends in Argentina said the government was anxious to discourage poachers, because the Patagonian region is so rich in fossil deposits."

"So they just let Steve go," Booker said, "instead of publicizing the incident to call attention to how easy it can be to poach things there."

"Exactly," Ling said. "Same as they usually do in China."

I shook my head. "Okay, so he can't go back to Argentina to dig, and we're going to make sure he can't ever show his face in Montana again," I said, ticking off places on my fingers. "Where's he off to at this point?"

Ling thought for a moment. "I think he's planning to head to China, which is really the best badlands for fossil finds right now. Steve can make a fortune there, between poaching bones in the poorest regions of the country, and faking all kinds of finds like he's trying to do here tonight."

I leaned back against the cold marble wall of the quiet corridor. "What a bad guy he is, Ling. Wow! He might have stopped you from getting your degree here."

There was a huge bang that jolted me out of my thoughts. I stood at the intersection of the two corridors and peeked around the corner.

I pulled back immediately and whispered to Booker and Ling. "It's Chip. He came out, slammed the lab door behind him, and now he's locking it."

"It hasn't been locked this whole time," Booker said.

"No one ever locks these doors," Ling said. "The museum is a community of scholars, and trust is at the core of it all. The president wouldn't have it any other way."

"That's okay," I said. "We basically have what we need to prove Ling's point."

"What if he's looking for *me*?" Ling asked, panicked at that idea. "I mean, not for the bones, but for me, personally?"

"Take it easy," I said. "He doesn't even know you're with us. Besides, he's walked off the other way."

"Chip must be going to tell Steve about the photographs he found on Dev's phone," Booker said, "and warn him that we were up here."

"What about my mother?" I asked, suddenly fearing that I wouldn't know if she texted back that she was on her way to help us. "She must be trying to reach me. Are you getting any bars on this side of the hallway?"

Booker and Ling both pulled out their phones. "Nothing," Booker said. "Maybe it's the storm."

The thunder booms sounded closer together now, as

though the worst of the action was centered right over the museum.

"How about I go downstairs and call your mom from there?" Booker asked. "I'll find out how close she is."

"Thanks, Booker. I owe you big time."

"I'll go downstairs with you, if you don't mind," Ling said.

I tensed up, even though I knew Chip had left the floor. "You're safe here with me, Ling."

"It just makes me feel—well—I don't want to be up here, near Steve's office."

"You feel safer with Booker, too," I said. "I get it."

"You can come, too," Booker said. "We can all go together. Chip did lock the door."

"I think I need to keep an eye on the lab," I said, gritting my teeth. "It's the center of Steve's entire operation. And he must have a key, also. Whatever kind of feathers he pasted to Katie's fossil are probably hidden inside there, too."

"You're not going to try to get in there again?" Booker asked.

"No way. I'm not anxious to get caught in the middle of Steve Paulson and Chip Donner," I said. "I just want to watch it, in case either one of them comes back. They can't get away with any of the faked fossils. You're only going downstairs to make a phone call, aren't you?"

"Or coming right back up with your mom," Booker said. "She might be here at the museum already, for all we know."

That was a calming thought.

"Okay," I said.

I sat down on the floor, out of the line of sight of the lab door. It was so still up here that I'd be able to hear anyone who came along.

I wondered if all the rooms around me were empty because the scientists who worked in this wing were at Steve Paulson's presentation. It was a totally phony PowerPoint, for sure.

I studied the dead birds stacked above one another in ceiling-high cases—each of them stuffed and staring back at me with beady eyes. They'd probably been stored up here for half a century.

I stood up again and started to pace, walking the length of the hallway toward the staircase that Booker and Ling had gone down just a minute ago. I tried to stay centered, and thought of the Rudyard Kipling poem I'd had to memorize for school.

I muttered the words, under my breath, to steady my nerves as I walked.

"If you can keep your head when all about you
Are losing theirs and blaming it on you, . . ."

I got through about three stanzas that I'd memorized, letting the poet's noble advice keep my spirits lifted.

There must have been a huge lightning strike nearby—although there were no windows on this hall for me to see it. But right before the next colossal crash of thunder shook me, the entire fifth floor shut down in darkness.

36

It's just a blackout, I told myself. It's just an electrical thing that would have to be restored within minutes.

The words of the poem flew out of my mind as I concentrated on what to do.

I didn't want to stand near the top of the staircase and take the chance of losing my footing and falling down in the dark.

If I could make my way back to the intersection of the two hallways, I would get to the turret that had windows facing out onto the museum's courtyard. They would provide some light.

I held my arms straight out in front of me as my eyes tried to adjust to the dark.

I took three careful steps forward, and then moved along more quickly. There was another loud sound—maybe a thunderclap—and I turned my head in case it was something inside the building, behind me. I almost lost my balance when I swiveled.

I continued my march forward in the dark, quickening my pace. But that sudden turn had thrown me off course.

My outstretched palms crashed up against an old wooden cabinet, twice as tall as I was. I felt it teetering as I slammed into it, and it fell over onto the floor, dumping its contents across the broad hallway as the glass panels shattered.

Suddenly the lights went back on. The museum's generator must have kicked in.

I had dropped to my knees on impact. Now I found myself surrounded by mounds of animals—dead animals. Creepy crawly rodents whose fur had collected dust over the years. Mice and rats and marmots and weasels. If there was a Pied Piper to be found anywhere, he'd missed this stash of unattractive creatures on his march out of town.

I cleared a path through the museum's collection of furry beings, dodging sharp shards of glass, and got to my feet, running toward the turret to make my escape.

37

I was racing through the hallway toward the turret, figuring that the route I knew best would take me down one flight to a security guard. I had no idea how far Booker and Ling had gone, in a direction unfamiliar to me, to make their phone call.

Halfway there, I heard voices. Two voices. Men talking to each other, getting louder as they climbed the staircase.

I had just passed the door to the lab, which I had watched Chip lock. I knew I'd bump right into the men—maybe the two I'd most wanted to avoid—if I kept going.

Then I thought of the pigeons that had come into the adjacent lab, seeking shelter, on Saturday night, scaring the wits out of me.

I ran to that door, twisted the handle, and pushed it open.

It was dark inside. Quiet and dark, rain still beating against the window. But no one was there, and I closed the door behind me, taking care not to bang it shut.

There was no bolt to lock it, and no sign of a key. So I just leaned against it to catch my breath.

I couldn't figure what was taking Booker and Ling so long—and my mother, too, for that matter. But now, if they returned to the hallway to look for me, they'd have no idea where I was hiding.

Footsteps and voices were getting closer now. The two men who were talking to each other were just a few feet away, in this very hallway.

I stood as still as I could—like a taxidermied grizzly bear in a museum exhibit, frozen in time and place. I tried to hold my breath.

The men stopped in front of the lab door. I could hear them clearly now. It was Steve Paulson and Chip Donner, and they were talking about me.

"That kid was a problem from the first day," Steve said. "I think she was out in Montana just digging for trouble."

Chip laughed. "I thought you threw them all off the scent when you created those tracks on the hillside during the night."

"Yeah," Steve said. "Me too. I figured that idea of poachers and trespassers would take those kids' minds off our real business."

"Too smart for their own good," Chip said. "I should have figured them for bad luck from the get-go."

"Give me your key," Steve said. "I'll show you where the bones are. Let's take 'em and get out of here while we can go."

The key rattled a bit and then the door opened. Both men walked inside and closed it behind them.

Their words were more muffled now and although I could hear movement in the room, I couldn't make out what they were saying.

The counter closest to the lab—the one that shared a wall with that room—was empty. I placed my foot on the stool next to it and boosted myself up. My sneakers made no noise as I positioned myself on the wooden planks.

I put my ear against the wall but couldn't hear much more.

Then I remembered one of my grandmother's favorite tricks. When she wanted to hear what the relatives were saying about her when they gathered at her apartment, she'd hold a drinking glass against the wall. Lulu had more practical advice for me than Rudyard Kipling ever would.

I leaned over and picked up an empty mason jar. It would do as well as a water glass.

I placed one end against the wall and the other to my ear.

"You don't think anyone in that conference room was suspicious, do you?" Chip asked.

"Not a chance. They're all so pumped up about getting the first shot at seeing a new species that if anyone opens his mouth, the rest will just claim he's jealous of me," Steve said.

"You're a patient man," Chip said, "holding on to those birdlike little legs for so long, just waiting for the right vertebrae fossil to come out of the earth."

It sounded like Steve was moving things around on the worktable, maybe packing up some fossils.

"I told you this work takes a lot of patience," Steve said. "I found them about a year ago."

"In Montana?" That was Chip asking the questions.

"Nope. South America."

Chip laughed. "So you've created a totally international dinosaur species."

"That will make it harder for paleontologists working here to catch on to my scam anytime soon," Steve said. "Got some feather-like extenders from China—bought them online—then some Patagonia juvenile leg bones and a Big Timber set of vertebrae."

"Done like a real pro."

"Had to be," Steve said. "It's the feathers attached to the vertebrae that gives the world a flying dinosaur. That's what makes our specimen so unique."

"You're keeping those pieces that Cion kid found, right?"

Steve didn't hesitate for a second. "Hey, we might want to give our Big Timber dino some cousins. Wouldn't want the old critter to get lonely."

"Good answer," Chip said. "I guess twenty years makes a lot of people forget what the Chinese tried to pull off back then."

"Sure does."

"And the equipment changes, too."

"My most important investment was in the glue, Chip. The newest glue won't even be detectable when they get to scans of my creation," Steve said. "That was one of the biggest problems the Chinese had way back when they tried to do something like this."

"Kind of like Dr. Frankenstein," Chip said. "You, making your own monster in a laboratory."

I could hardly believe my ears, but they had always been my greatest asset.

"Glad I got you on board," Steve said. "You were pretty reluctant when I asked you to join in with me."

"I've never done anything illegal," Chip said, lowering

his voice. "But then, nobody ever gave me the chance to strike it rich before you did."

"I'm almost ready to go," Steve said. "I've got everything except the most important piece of the puzzle. Can't leave those behind."

I could hear footsteps as Steve walked toward the far side of the room.

The men seemed to be moving items around on the shelves, but neither of them spoke. Then Steve broke the silence, slamming something—maybe his hand—against the counter.

"They're not here, Chip!" Steve said, shouting at his companion. "I'm telling you this is exactly where I left those fossils the Cion kid found. And we need to get them out of the museum tonight so that they're with me when I fly out of town in the morning."

"Don't look at me. I never touched them," Chip said. "Where else could they be?"

"Who did you say was with that devil girl when she was in here a bit ago?"

"Devlin, Steve. Her name is Devlin."

"I know her name, and I know I'd like to wring her skinny neck if I could catch up with her about now," Steve said.

I recoiled, holding on to the glass so I didn't drop it.

“They’re gone,” Chip said. “I think I scared them out of here.”

“Don’t you get it, Chip?” Steve said, raising his voice so much that I didn’t need the jar. “That kid’s mother is the police commissioner. If that woman shows up—if those kids got their hands on the fossils—you and I will be digging our own way out of jail, instead of making our fortune in China.”

I had to get out of this place. I slipped down off the counter, leaving the jar right where I’d found it.

Chip opened the door of the lab. I could hear him shout back to Steve from the corridor. “I’ll go look for the kids. Could be they’re still in the museum.”

He passed by my safe room and headed for the staircase in the turret. There was no way I could follow him at this point, and I didn’t want to go back and play slip’n’slide with the dead rodents laid out in the other direction. Dead or alive, they totally creeped me out, and I had no idea what else lurked in that direction.

Now I realized what it felt like to be trapped. I had a whole new respect for all the animals that had been tracked down, hunted, killed, and then stuffed, to spend eternity in a museum. No disrespect to Teddy Roosevelt, but I wasn’t ever going to be a fan of any hunters.

I picked up the jar again and leaned over the counter to hear what Steve was up to. He seemed to be moving more things around on shelves.

Then he stepped into the hallway, coming back to the counter, sort of talking to himself before he slammed the door shut behind him. "Footprints. Dusty footprints," he said to himself. "Somebody else is skulking around up here."

That would be *me*! I must have tracked decades of dust from the storage cases of rodents that I'd overturned. If Steve went back to look at the prints—if he paid them any more attention—he'd see they led right into this room.

I had to act fast. This was no place to have a confrontation with an angry criminal desperate to get his hands on the evidence of his guilt—and on my neck.

The idea came to me in a flash, with the next thunderclap. It wasn't a pretty thought, but I could thank my friend Katie—and those trespassing pigeons—for holding out hope of a route to safety.

38

I took off my sneakers and socks. This was a job for bare feet. Slipping was not in the cards.

Then I opened the door as quietly as I could.

Yup, dusty prints led right into this room. I kneeled down and looked out into the hallway. With my hands stuffed inside my sneakers, I made a set of tracks leading away from my position, reaching over each step and stretching my arms as far as I could to lay down another one.

Then I sat up, crawled away, stood to close the door behind me. I tucked my sneakers and socks as far out of sight as they would go under the workbench.

I went to the end of the room, climbed up once again, and pulled open the handle on the old casement window.

The rain was still coming down, but not as fiercely as it had been at the height of the storm. It was a summer rain, too, so it wasn't too cold.

I don't like heights that much. I had no problem looking out from the top of a skyscraper, but walking on window ledges? That's not entirely my thing. Maybe that's why I'd never tried it before.

It must have been five o'clock in the afternoon. Streetlights had come on early because of the dark clouds and heavy rain.

I could see that the ledge was about a foot wide just outside the window I had opened. And I knew from scores of museum visits that the turrets were covered with carved animals—fantastic sculptures that represented most of the creatures on display in cases below.

Now all I had to do was get from this windowsill to the turret, and cling to the neck of one of those animals until I was out of danger.

But that seemed to me, at the moment, like walking a tightrope across the Grand Canyon without a net.

I had to stop shaking before I could move, but telling myself that just made it worse for me.

Then I heard Steve, yelling down the corridor to Chip. "Check out the footprints! Don't look big enough to be a grown man's, do they?"

I couldn't bring myself to step out on the ledge. Maybe the guys would fall for my fake sneaker marks. No reason to try a high-wire act if I didn't need to.

Chip must have doubled back to where Steve was standing, right in front of the door to this room.

They were whispering to each other now, and I couldn't make out the words. I froze in place with my back against the heavy window, trying hard to hold my breath. It seemed to me that even if I exhaled, the men would hear the sound.

Dead quiet for thirty seconds.

Then I could see the knob twist. My stomach knotted up as the door pushed in.

"Eureka!" Steve said. "Looks like we've got our culprit, doesn't it?"

"You don't have anything," I said. "Once they do a CT scan of your phony fossil, everyone will know the truth."

Steve shook his head at me. "Not with my miracle glue. So far, it's fooled every machine we've practiced on."

"You won't fool President Sutton," I said.

"Bring her down and then we'll figure out what to do with her," Steve said.

Chip charged toward me, his arms out in front as though he was going to grab my legs

"Oh, no you don't," I said, aiming my foot at his head but missing the mark.

Chip lunged again but I had steadied myself and put the same leg through the opening and out onto the windowsill.

Time for me to channel my grandmother. "Never look

back, Dev," Lulu liked to say to me. "You may spot someone you don't want to see coming after you."

"Where do you think you're going?" Steve yelled.

I stepped out onto the ledge and took a minute to balance myself. I think Lulu's advice was a reference to my swimming competitions, but it might hold me in good stead up here.

I could see Chip's head peeking out through the window, but I knew anyone much larger than I was would have a hard time balancing on this ledge.

When I had firm footing, I stood on my tiptoes and swiveled to face the building, clinging to a narrow strip of cement that jutted out all along the side at about the height of my shoulder.

"Go after her," Steve yelled.

"No way I can," Chip said. "But I can make sure Dev's only got one way to go, other than straight down."

"What?" Steve asked.

"Go to the next office over and we'll grab her as she tries to pass it," Chip said.

I didn't know if I could summon the courage to make it that far. But the men left me little choice. The window I'd stepped out of slammed behind me, and I heard the old metal lock turn in place.

This time, there was no turning back.

39

I stepped carefully to my right, toward the turret about twenty feet away, I could see a light go on in the room I had just exited.

I didn't look down once. If there were people in the interior courtyard of the museum below me, I didn't want to see them until I could get to a secure perch.

I took a minute to get my bearings. All that I had to lean against was the wall of the building. The roof sloped away from me, somewhere up above. The height was dizzying—it may have been the fifth floor of the museum, but each one was double or triple height—so it was as though I was looking down from the tenth floor of a high-rise.

I couldn't make out any individuals on the pavement below. The people didn't exactly look like ants, but no bigger than caterpillars.

The sky still looked dark and threatening, and heaven seemed closer to me than earth.

Inch by inch, I made my way along the ledge, scraping my nose against the old brick facade of the museum as

I turned my head to the side to look for the giant cone-shaped turret.

I kept looking back, even though I knew I shouldn't, thinking Chip might try to catch up with me after all.

My hands and feet were sopping wet, and rain was dripping off my head, soaking my clothes.

"Don't look back," I repeated to myself. "Don't ever look down. One foot at a time."

The tip of my nose was bleeding now. I had turned my head so many times—maybe fifteen already—that I couldn't help but rub the skin off it against the brick of the museum wall.

I tried to think of Mary Poppins and Bert the chimney sweep and all the other characters in literature I loved who had made it safely across rooftops, smiling as they scaled the heights and balanced on drainpipes.

It was just another few steps. I had never been the best dancer in my ballet class, but I could hold my own on a balance beam if I needed to. And this was the moment to land a perfect score.

One more look to my right. There it was—a most majestic sight. It was a statue of an eagle—a great soaring bald eagle—that guarded the turret of the museum and was the most welcoming creature in sight.

I took two more steps toward the giant bird, reaching

out for him with my right hand, stepping one foot on top of his spread claw and swinging myself onto his body, burying my wet face against his firm back.

I was high over the streets of Manhattan, safely nestled between the carved wings of the magnificent eagle.

40

Two minutes later, the window I had escaped from opened. I lifted my head, my heart pounding in my chest, expecting Steve or Chip to appear and continue to try to catch me.

But the voice I heard was neither of theirs.

"Dev! Devlin Quick!" my mother shouted. Time for the full first name approach, not that I could blame her. "Are you—?"

"I'm okay, Mom," I said, fighting back tears. "I'm really okay."

"I love you, Dev. Everything's going to be fine, baby."

I usually hated it when she called me 'baby,' but boy was I happy to hear it now.

"Hang on, Dev. Can you do that for me?"

I was too choked up to talk. I wanted to ask if she'd caught Steve and if Ling was okay and most of all, how she intended to get me down off this giant bird and into her arms.

I shook my head up and down.

"I called you, Mom," I said. "I really did."

"I know that, Dev," my mother said. "And Booker told us the rest."

"How'd you find me?"

"I'm the police commissioner. What good would I be if I couldn't find you?"

"But here?"

"Booker told us where they had left you, on the fifth floor," my mom said. "And when we got up there, we caught Steve and Chip running away—out of this room."

I closed my eyes and tried to stay strong.

"I'm sorry it took us so long," she said. "I'm so sorry."

I was trembling again, frightened and dripping wet. "Not your fault, Mom."

"Can you hold on to the bird, Dev? Can you hold on for just a little longer?"

I was clinging to the great winged creature with everything I had in me

"No problem," I said.

"Can you hear that siren, down on the street?" she called out. She was sitting in the window now, one leg out on the sill.

"Yes. Yes, I do."

"That's a fire truck," she said. "Sam's going down to the street right below you, to wait for the fire truck."

It was making me panicky to look down. I felt safe against the strong body of the eagle, but I also wanted to see my mother's face, to know she was all right. I know how she worries about me under the best of circumstances.

"No, no—don't turn your head. Stay straight. The firemen will help get you right to Sam."

"Will you be there, Mom? I need you to be there."

"Sam's stronger than I am, Dev. I'm just keeping my eye on you till they bring you down. I need to be where I can see you till they get you on the ground."

"But Steve and Chip, Mom," I said. "They were going to try to catch me right behind here, in the turret."

"Steve and Chip are in custody, I promise you," my mother said. "We've got them right where we want them."

I rested my head on the eagle's back again.

I still didn't dare to look down, but I could hear the siren and I knew that the truck must have come to a stop right below me.

One of the fireman had a loudspeaker. He pointed it skyward to talk to me.

"Devlin Quick! Hook and Ladder Company Number Four. We're coming to get you to safety."

"She's good," my mother said, giving the battalion chief a thumbs-up.

I watched as the ladder slowly extended from the street right up to the side of the eagle, with a sturdy fireman standing inside a bucket that was large enough to hold me, too.

"Hey there, Dev," he said as he pulled into view. "I'm Pudge. I understand you just added another bad guy to your list of arrests."

I gave him a weak smile in return.

"What you're going to do when I get real close is put that right arm around my neck," he said. "Just lock it there, and I'm going to do all the rest."

"I can barely think, sir," I said.

"You don't have to think right now. Just give me the tightest squeeze you've got in you, and then I'm going to wrap this belt around you, too."

I followed directions and grabbed on to him, probably harder than he expected. It's a good thing he didn't have a skinny neck like me.

"Close your eyes, Dev, if you're afraid of heights."

"I used to be, but I don't think I am anymore," I said. I almost managed a laugh.

Pudge had one of his powerful arms around me,

along with a safety harness. He lifted me off my winged chariot and into his bucket. I was holding on to him so fiercely that I thought my fingers were going to break in half.

Once in the bucket, I didn't close my eyes for a moment. First I looked back at my mother and blew her a kiss. Then I looked down at the fire truck and its flashing lights, which had attracted quite a crowd.

I couldn't make out any faces, but what had looked like ants and caterpillars from my perch began to take on human forms as we got lower and lower. Pudge had his arms around me for the entire trip as the bucket rattled and shuddered on its way to the ground.

Someone steering our bucket from the truck was slow and steady, and I began to breathe more easily as we came closer to the street.

The first person I recognized was Sam, who was craning his neck to look up at me, and had taken hold of the megaphone.

"Cruising down to me, Devlin Quick," Sam said. "Slow and steady wins the race."

The bucket came to a stop. I was never so happy to see a New York City sidewalk.

"I'm passing the hero over to you, Sam," Pudge said, helping me out of the large steel box that had shuttled me to safety. "Better take good care of this girl or I'll be back to get you."

"I've got no choice in that matter," Sam said, grabbing on to me to pull me close to his side, and then stepping back to wrap me in a warm blanket. "She's my number one partner, Pudge. Devlin Quick's the best sleuth in town."

41

President Sutton had an office that was almost as cool as my mother's suite in the Puzzle Palace. It was perfectly round, and decorated with wonderful treasures from every branch of her great museum.

She had given me a sweatshirt and pants from the museum shop, covered with glittery creatures that glowed in the dark. Unfortunately for me, they were all dinosaurs—the last beasts I wanted to see at the moment. It wasn't exactly a fashion statement, but it was a lot better than my wet clothes.

"I didn't mean to leave you alone up there," Booker said.

"I know that," I said, resting my head in my mother's lap, stretched out on the sofa in President Sutton's suite.

"I just went to call Aunt Blaine, and when I got her, she was only a couple of blocks from the museum."

"I asked Booker to wait for us," my mother said. "Otherwise, he would have been back up to you much sooner."

"Don't you both be so apologetic," I said. "I knew you'd get to me as soon as you could."

"I just have to tell you—" my mother started to say, before I interrupted.

"Can we save the lecture for tomorrow, Mom?" I asked.

"There isn't going to be any lecture," she said.

I knew it would make her feel good to stroke my hair and kiss the tip of my wounded nose, so I let her do it. I kind of liked being coddled myself, right at that moment.

"Really?" I asked, looking up at her as she rubbed my cheek.

"Your Atwell ears are a genetic treasure, Dev," my mother said. "But we've all been overlooking your keen sense of smell."

I squinted and sniffed a few times. "What do you mean?"

"The way you seem to smell injustice, Dev. It's sort of uncanny," my mother said, "and this isn't the first time you've done it."

"Katie did, too."

"Of course she did. And each of you stuck with it, sensing that something was very wrong, even though you couldn't pinpoint what it was."

"We told all the adults, Mom," I said. "You and Mrs. Cion and everyone we could that what went on in Montana just didn't seem right to us."

"No question about that," Sam said. "A good sniffer, the right instincts, and a healthy dab of courage make a great detective, Devlin."

"I'm working on the courage part," I said.

"You've got a boatload of it. Just don't use it all in one place, okay?"

"Promise," I said. "Where's Ling?"

"She's with President Sutton," my mother said. "Preparing for a press conference. A brand-new one. And she's already been promised readmission to her program at Yale."

"That's amazing," I said. "Booker—we can visit her there."

"Cool," Booker said. "Is President Sutton going to tell the public the truth about the fossils, Aunt Blaine?"

"Of course she is," my mother said. "With Ling at her side."

I held on to my mother's hand to get my nerve up to ask the next question. "Steve and Chip will be in jail, right?"

"We're making dino digs safer for everyone, Devlin," Sam said.

"They're charged with Forgery in the First Degree and Criminal Possession of Stolen Property," my mother said, "for the other fossils they were running off with. Yes, once they're convicted, they'll go to jail."

I sat up and pumped my fist in the air. "Then the clutch of eggs is still the Ditch, and the super-duck is going to be named Willie, for Miss Ditchley," I said. "And Katie Cion is still king of the hillside."

"When all is said and done," my mother said, "there may well be a species called the *Cionosaurus katus* after all."

"So Katie will still have the best birthday present ever," I said.

"You two didn't just solve a crime," my mother said to Booker and me. "You also got to the bottom of all this by using your brains—"

"And my mom's CT scan machine," Booker said, flashing his Dibble-dazzle smile.

"That, too," my mother said, smiling back. "You uncovered a hoax that would have been played out all around the world—in great museums and against scientists doing their best to make important finds available to the public, to expand their knowledge of paleontology. You did a very important thing."

"Hocus-pocus," Sam said, pulling me up on my feet.

"With a little bit of magic, I bet we can turn you into a thoroughly dry twelve-year-old who belongs at home with a takeout pizza followed by an early bedtime. No scary stories tonight."

"Wait a minute," I said. "Why did you say 'hocus-pocus' just now?"

"'Cause I plan to work some magic on you. Clean you up and get you out of this crime scene. That's where the word 'hoax' comes from, Devlin," Sam said. "The old chant magicians used centuries ago, to blind the eye of the beholder and pass off a stunt that they hoped wouldn't get noticed as a fake. That's the reason they're called hoaxes."

"Like Steve's faked fossils," I said. "Hocus-pocus. I guess he figured Katie and I wouldn't ever know we'd been tricked."

"Steve tried to fool many more people than just you kids," my mother said. "He tried to deceive all the bone diggers in the world."

"Move over, T. rex," Sam Cody said, putting his Windbreaker around my shoulders to lead us out to his car to take us home. "It took *Tyrannosaurus dev* to break the case. You're a fearsome leader, young lady, and a strong one."

My mother and Booker locked arms and walked with

us. "Now it's time to put this caper behind you," she said to me. "Understand that?"

"I'll have to testify for the district attorney, Mom, won't I?"

"I bet they can build a really strong case without you, Devlin Quick," my mother said. "You and Booker saved the day when you found that bag of bones."

"Katie's bones," I said, yawning, safe in the company of my extended family. "All I want to do now is crawl into my bed."

"Hocus-pocus," Sam said, grabbing my hand in his. "I'll have you home faster than you can say Teddy Roosevelt."

"Not him!" I said.

"Forget I mentioned his name," Sam said, walking hand in hand with me. "You've got me, and you've got the commissioner of the NYPD. What more do you need?"

"Not a thing," I said. "It's just where Booker and Katie and I want to be, on the front lines, fighting crime."

"I'm counting on seeing you there, Devlin Quick," Sam said. "And we'll always have your back."

-ACKNOWLEDGMENTS-

It seems to me that everyone loves dinosaurs, so digging for fossils was an adventure I wanted to enjoy along with Devlin Quick.

To get up to speed, I went to one of my favorite places in the world—the American Museum of Natural History. It was there I met my first dinos when I was a kid, and I return often to learn about new discoveries. I am very grateful for the access made possible by the brilliant and dynamic Ellen Futter, president of the museum, who has created such a first-rate institution. It's always a joy to visit—whether in person or online.

Michael Novacek is the Chief Curator of Paleontology at AMNH, and gave me a crash course in fossil digs. His book—*Dinosaurs of the Flaming Cliffs*—was my guide through rough, new terrain. His Research Assistant Suzann Goldberg provided me with wonderful details and a true sense of desert searches.

The Museum of the Rockies in Bozeman, Montana, is another great place to get to know dinosaurs. Recently retired Curator of Paleontology, Jack Horner, knows that turf well, and his book—*Dinosaurs Under the Big Sky*—showed me the western way to dig.

I admire the librarians, teachers, and booksellers who introduce readers to Devlin and Booker, and I'm still hoping to turn up a dinosaur bone of my own when I'm kicking around the ranch in Big Timber.